Mercy, Unbound

KIM ANTIEAU

SIMON PULSE
New York   London   Toronto   Sydney

SIMON PULSE

An imprint of Simon & Schuster Children's Publishing Division
1230 Avenue of the Americas, New York, NY 10020
Copyright © 2006 by Kim Antieau
All rights reserved, including the right of reproduction in whole or in part in any form.
SIMON PULSE and colophon are registered trademarks of Simon & Schuster, Inc.
Designed by Debra Sfetsios
The text of this book was set in Bembo Italic and Futura Book.
Manufactured in the United States of America
First Simon Pulse edition May 2006
2 4 6 8 10 9 7 5 3 1
Library of Congress Control Number 2005924378
ISBN-13: 978-1-4169-0893-7
ISBN-10: 1-4169-0893-5

Mercy, Unbound

for michelle

Mercy,
Unbound

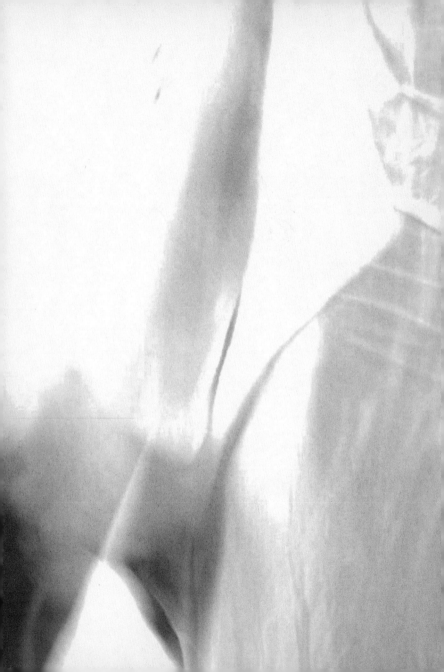

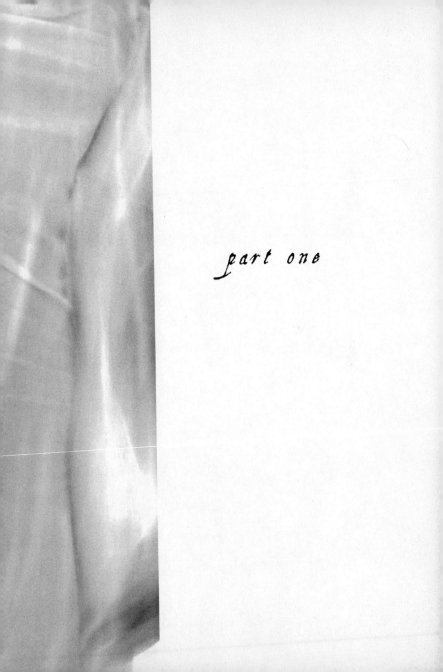

part one

Call me Mercy. Or TAM for short. T.he A.ngel M.ercy. Yes, I'm an angel. Or about to be an angel. I have only recently awakened to this realization. Or figured it out. A revelation, if you will. The wings were a big clue. You can't see them? You will. At first they felt like new teeth coming in. Do you remember that feeling? Kind of itchy, irritating. I wanted to cry all the time. I lost my appetite. Then I knew. Those little buds on my shoulder blades— along with everything else—sealed the deal. I was an angel. And angels don't need to eat.

"You're not an angel, Mercy. You're a fifteen-year-old girl! A young woman. You have to eat. It's dinnertime. I should have never named you Mercy. What were we thinking? We weren't, actually, since I was in labor. George said, 'Let's call her Mercy, because God is merciful,' and I screamed, 'Cut the crap, George! Oh, lord have mercy!' It was purely coincidental, really. I wasn't calling out your

3

name, I was just trying not to swear too much. We were in a Catholic hospital, and I didn't want to offend. George, talk to your daughter. She needs to come down here and eat!"

That was my mother. When she's scared, she gets angry. A defense mechanism, my father says. I think she's funny. Most of the time. But she doesn't understand that silence can be golden. I think she talks a lot because then she knows she is breathing. She has asthma, and sometimes she can't talk much because she's out of breath—so talking is just her way of letting the world know she's still alive and kicking.

"Goddamn it, George. If she doesn't eat, she's gonna waste away."

"You can't force her to eat."

"I will not watch my daughter starve. Mercy!"

For not believing in God, my mom sure does take God's name in vain a lot. I'm purposely not using a pronoun—he or she— because I don't see God as a he or a she. Really. I never have. OK. That's not quite right. Sometimes when I'm outside in the woods and see a cardinal (no pun on the name intended) all bright and red, sitting on the branch of an oak tree, I'll think, "Isn't he beautiful." And I know that the cardinal is God. Or the next-door neighbor's cat, Muncie, who is a calico, she'll look at me a certain way, and I'll have to laugh, because I know she is God.

I used to be sad all the time. Then something happened.

But that's a different story. I was talking about my mother. She doesn't believe in God. She said she can't because if there really was a God who could make things better and didn't, then that God was a crazy evil sonofabitch—and she would not could not believe in that kind of God.

"What about a God who isn't omnipotent?" I asked her once. "What if God was just this creative being who now needs a little help? What would you say to that?"

"I'd say to God, 'We've all got problems, buddy. Get in line.'"

"Mercy."

My father is so different from my mother. Night and day. And he's the day. Laid back. Nonconfrontational. Calm. But then, my mother says, he has reason to be. He was raised in the Midwest on a farm—an organic farm, no less—by calm and loving parents who provided for him and his sister and brother. When I was a girl, before I knew I was an angel, my father would let me crawl all over him. When I was very little, he would sit on the floor of my bedroom with me and play for hours. He would do whatever I asked. Play whatever game I wanted to play. When Mom was pregnant with my brother, we played "baby in the tummy" for months.

Only the baby in the tummy never got birthed. They took him out after he died. At least that was what my parents told

5

me later. Or maybe Grandma told me. I'm not sure. They never talk about it now. His name was Peter. That's all I know. That and the fact that he sat at the end of my bed for a few years after he wasn't born. I never told Mom and Dad. I think that would have sent Mom right over the edge.

"Mercy," my father said again. "You have to eat."

"I'm not hungry, Dad," I said.

"Please, come down to the table," he said. "This can't be good for you, and it's very upsetting to your mother."

I acquiesce. Dad puts his arm across my shoulder as we start down the stairs, then quickly draws away from me.

"How much weight have you lost?" he asks.

"How many angels can fit on the head of a pin?" I ask.

"Mercy—"

"Angels don't weigh anything at all," I say. "Don't worry. It's like we angels are on the Moon all the time. Think of us as Earth astronauts, George."

My father sighs. He does not like it when I call him George, but he's not really my father. At least I don't think he is. Any more than Nancy is really my mother. Angels don't have parents, do they?

"I wish you'd call me Dad," he says, again. "I'm sure angels have parents."

"Only dead ones," I say.

"Pardon me?" *We are walking into the dining room now.*

The long walnut table has been set for three. Bowls of food with steam rising from them decorate the table. I don't pay any attention to what is in the bowls. Unfortunately, I still crave earthly delights and must constantly monitor myself.

"Children can become angels," I say, "if they're dead. So I'm saying I could have parents if I were a child."

My mother comes into the dining room then. She's heard what I said, and she looks stunned.

"I was just explaining—"

"Sit down and eat," Mom says. "All of you."

I guess by "all of us" she means my dad and me. Although I don't know for certain. Ghosts seem to haunt our dinner table.

"Mercy, you have to eat something besides salt," my mother said.

"Leave her alone," George said gently.

"You want her to starve to death?"

"Don't they have angels in the Jewish faith?" I asked.

"I don't know," Mom said. "Ask a Jew who has some faith."

Mom and Dad eat silently. I lick my finger, press it against the salt I've poured out onto my mom's blue and white china, then bring the salt to my tongue. I don't know why I crave it. I look around and see the golden chest they used to lock with a chain and padlock every night. Inside they put a treasure trove of all the food I binged on: loaves of bread, pasta, cookies, cake mixes,

*etc. They don't lock it anymore. They leave it wide open, as a
kind of invitation to eat. They don't understand. I binged when
I was sad. I'm not sad anymore.*

My mother dropped her fork. It clattered against the
china, kind of echoing around the dining room.

"I dieted once when I was in high school," she said.
"Once. I thought I was fat. When I complained to my
mother, she slapped me across the face. And do you
know what she said then? 'Look around, sister. You
don't see a grandmother, do you? You don't see an aunt
or uncle, no cousins. No grandfather. Do you know
why? Because they're all dead! They starved to death
in Nazi concentration camps. So don't you dare dis-
honor their memory by not eating. You eat! And you eat
well. You are eating for your entire family!' That was
the last time I ever complained. Last time I ever dieted.
Now you, Mercy, you must eat."

"I'm not dieting, Mom. I promise you. I just don't
need to eat."

"That's it," my mother said, standing. "I'm calling Dr.
Perkins. We're taking you to Mercywood."

*My mother does not see the irony of taking me to a hospital
called Mercywood. Sometimes I imagine what it must be like at
Mercywood. It has a wonderful-sounding name, doesn't it? Do
you think perhaps it is surrounded by a dark and wild forest,*

just for me? But it's in the Southwest. They don't have the kind of forests I was thinking of—you know, huge old oaks and maples. Those kinds of trees feel solid, don't they? Like they really hold the wisdom of the ages. What do they have in the Southwest? Piñon scrub? Juniper. I vaguely remember stories about juniper trees. I read a book once by Kate Wilhelm called Juniper Time. *Didn't she say something about juniper trees? They live forever, I think. That book takes place on the Oregon coast. I've never been there, but I imagine it must be full of huge old gnarled trees, standing for centuries against the rain, wind, and time. Don't they have redwood forests there? Huge Douglas firs. Or have they cut them all down?*

I asked my father what the ocean feels like—you know, standing there as the waves come in and go out—and he said feeling the spray on his face was like getting kissed by a fairy. "Unless it's windy," he said, "then it feels like being licked by Sandy." Sandy is our dog. Was our dog. She was hit by a car and died.

Anyway, Mercywood is not on the Oregon coast or any other coast. I read somewhere that the whole Southwest desert was once under water—part of the ocean. Do you think it remembers? The land, I mean. The Southwest always seems a bit haunted, doesn't it? I said that earlier, about our dining-room table—not the table exactly, but our sitting around it, eating. Or trying to eat.

We visited New Mexico twice, once over Christmas vacation. I don't remember much about the Xmas trip or anything about the other one. I was a kid then. I remember seeing these paper bags everywhere, set over lights. I didn't really understand why they did that. But it was pretty. I remember Mom had a hard time breathing. Something about the altitude. She kept saying she had to acclimate. When I asked what that meant, my father said, "She has to get used to the place. It's very high here, like where the birds fly. So there's not a lot of air." I breathed deeply, trying to tell the difference between the air here and the air in Michigan, where we lived, and I could not discern a difference, except at home the air smelled wet; in the desert it smelled dry. When I told my parents this, they laughed and asked me to explain. I couldn't. I knew what I meant, but I didn't know how to tell them what I meant. For Christmas breakfast we ate at a place called Cafe Pasqual's, and I had something with fried banana in it. I can't remember if I liked it, but I had to have it as soon as my dad told me it was on the menu. Was it part of an omelet or fried eggs? I don't know. My mom said, "If you get it, you're going to eat it." She bit her lip right after she said it. She does that a lot now. But I remember it then, almost as though it was the first time I noticed it. And I knew she wished she had not said what she said. "I'll eat the whole thing," I promised. "That's all right, darling," Mom said. "You can eat as little or as much as you like."

I liked Cafe Pasqual's. It was named after Saint Pasqual, saint of the kitchen, my dad read from the menu.

"How can a man be the saint of a kitchen?" my mom asked.

"Just like the Catholic Church to make a man the saint of a kitchen. How many men do you know cook?"

"Daddy," I said. "Daddy cooks." Which was true. My mother had stopped cooking, pretty much, after the baby in the tummy wasn't born. Mom and Dad had cooked together before that—at least that's how I remember it. My grandma Dottie—my mom's mom—used to kick Dad out of the kitchen during the holidays. She'd switch him on the bottom with some kitchen utensil and tell him the kitchen was no place for him. But he insisted, explaining to Grandma that they wanted me to grow up without gender prejudices. Grandma would roll her eyes and say they weren't "gender prejudices," whatever that was. It was just the way things were, but after a while she gave in. Now she even seems to enjoy Dad's company and will kick Mom out of the kitchen. She moved to Florida last winter. I haven't seen her in months.

My mom's dad, Grandpa Max, died when I was little. He was one of the liberators, one of the Americans who went to the camps. He smelled like pipe tobacco. He had a big belly, usually covered by a vest with a gold pocket watch tucked into one of the small pockets. I loved sitting on his lap and listening to his heart beat—and playing with the pocket watch. Very carefully. He would open it up, and I could see all the gears moving back and forth as the second hand went around and around. It was like looking at someone's heart, I thought.

Grandpa Max liked watching television, especially old movies. Since we didn't have TV at our house, it was a special treat to go to Grandpa Max and Grandma Dottie's house to watch movies with Grandpa Max. When he laughed, I would bounce up and down on his lap. I told Mom I thought Grandpa Max was the real Santa Claus. She looked over at Grandma Dottie when I told her this and asked, "Can Santa be Jewish?"

My mom said Grandpa Max never got over the horrors he saw when he helped liberate the camp. How could anyone? To see dead people walking around this camp. He dreamed about it all the rest of his life. He found Grandma Dottie there that day, the day of the liberation. Gave her a flower he had found outside the camp. At least that was the story Grandma Dottie always told.

Funny how they call it a camp. Like it was some place people went for summer vacation. Or to be out in the country. Why didn't they call it a concentration death house? And why concentration? I'll have to look that up. I don't think I ever really thought about it before this moment. This may explain why I didn't want to go to summer camp when I was a kid. Every time Mom and Dad brought it up, I'd scream to high heaven and they'd drop it. Did I think Mom and Dad were sending me to a concentration camp?

But we were talking about me going to Mercywood. I don't know why I keep trotting down memory lane. It doesn't matter to me if I go to Mercywood or not. In fact, it could be just the thing. I'm an angel. I should be helping people. What better place than a hospital—even if it is a hospital dedicated to people with eating disorders? I remember what it was like to

be obsessed with food. Sort of. But it won't matter whether I
remember or not. I can still help.

"She's blue, my husband," my mother said, trying to
convince my dad that I should go to the hospital. "Have
you noticed that? Her skin is nearly translucent. She's
blue—like she's always cold. Last week she was having
tunnel vision. Did she tell you that? She was crying and
screaming she was so afraid. I took her to the doctor.
She didn't want me to tell you, so you wouldn't worry,
but you need to worry. People die from this. Then we'd
be orphans, or whatever it's called. Is there a word?
When you have children and then you don't? There's got
to be a word."

"We don't know these people at Mercywood," Dad
said. "She'd be so far from home."

"Like home has helped her. You've met the staff at
Mercywood. They're good, and it's a beautiful facility."

My mother was a bear, and she'd say or do anything
to protect her cub. She didn't realize I was not in harm's
way—becoming an angel would protect me. And then
maybe I could fix some of the problems of the world.

*They're talking softly now, so I can't hear them. I think I hear
Sandy outside barking, but then I remember she's dead. Do
dogs become angels?*

Mom and Dad talked to me after they visited Mercywood.

In Dr. Perkins's office. They told me if they took me to Mercywood and I didn't eat, they would force me to eat. They wouldn't shove the food down my throat or anything, Dr. Perkins reassured me. They would give me food via an IV. Not quite so barbaric.

I started to cry. I pleaded with Dr. Perkins to understand that I was an angel. "Becoming an angel," I said, "if you like that better. If I eat, it won't work. I'll lose my wings." Then the three adults looked at one another like I had said exactly the thing they knew I would say. The crazy thing.

I've been going to Dr. Perkins for a year. She is very sweet. It was nice to talk to her about Sandy when she died and when Grandma moved. But she thinks there is some underlying psychological reason that I'm not eating. She won't listen. No one is really listening to me.

Peter used to listen. Those couple of years when he was an angel sitting on the end of my bed. It's funny, when I think about it, because he died before he was born, but at the end of my bed he was about ten years old, wearing shorts and a striped red and black shirt, open at the collar. A white collar. I would tell him about my day at school, or what Sandy and I had seen in the woods, or what movie Mom and Dad had taken me to. He never seemed resentful; I didn't feel guilty because he couldn't do all the things I could do. Sometimes I would tell him about something at school—a test, a baseball game, a fight—and he'd say, "Good job," like Mom and Dad did, only there wasn't anything else wrapped up in those two

14

words like there was when my parents said them. I always felt like they wanted to say, "Good girl," but someone had told them once it was tantamount to child abuse, so they never would, never did, equate my actions with my being a "good" girl or not. But I knew, just as every child knows, that my parents wanted me to be good. And goodness is definitely strictly in the eye and mind of the beholder—i.e., the parent.

Not that I'm whining about my treatment. I know I am very lucky. I know I have it better than most of the world. I know that millions of children have been orphaned because their parents have died of AIDS. They mostly live in Africa, and they have nothing and no one to care for them. Millions of them. What would that be like? I know I cannot imagine it. Sometimes when I try to imagine it, I think of my grandma in Ravensbrück, sixteen years old, watching her mother wither away from starvation. Until she was alone. And now these AIDS orphans in Africa are wandering around alone in the wilderness and in cities—without a soul to care for them. One of the kids in class said she heard that in Africa even guardian angels die of AIDS. That scared me. What if guardian angels really can die of AIDS? Something must have happened, because so many are dying.

I'm really hungry. I have to be honest here and admit it. As I'm writing this, I'm starving. Although I know it's obscene for me even to think something like that. I am a perfectly healthy, well-fed American teenager.

There is medicine now to help people with AIDS. But it's not *getting to the people who need it. So millions of people are dying.*

Millions of people.

You see, that's why we need angels. We need millions of angels. Then we'll be able to do something. We'll be able to help. But unless I stop eating, unless I get over this urge to consume, I won't ever become a full-blooded angel. I mean, look at me now; hardly anyone can see my wings.

And my parents think I'm crazy.

"Some people are trying to force us back to the days when women had no rights over their own bodies," my mother said after she printed out the AIDS information for a paper I was doing. "That's essentially what they're doing in Africa. Denying women their reproductive rights. Here in the United States women died so that other women could have the same rights as men."

"I know," I said. "The suffragists."

She nodded. "They went on hunger strikes. The prison guards force-fed them. Some of them died. And other women were arrested for distributing information about birth control to poor women. Margaret Sanger. They were amazing women. They changed the world by refusing to eat."

This was when I was first "having the trouble," and as soon as my mother uttered that last sentence, she bit her lip.

"Is that what you're doing?" she asked. "Are you making some kind of political statement by not eating? Or by eating and then throwing it all up?"

"No, Mom," I said. "I just get really hungry sometimes.

And then I'm not hungry anymore. I feel contaminated. Or something. Like I've just got to get it out of me before something bad happens."

"And what 'something bad' would that be?"

I shrugged. "I don't know. I've never let it go that far. If I feel that way, I throw it up and I feel better."

"Let's just stop talking about it," my dad said quietly downstairs. Did I say he's a teacher? Literature. At Eastern Michigan University. Pray-Harrold. That's where his offices are and where he teaches. When I was younger, I used to think we had to pray to Harrold before going into the building.

"We talk about food all the time," he said. "And we're always talking about bad things. Politics. The environment. Immigration. There's just too much information floating around this house."

My mother laughed. "You think ignorance equals bliss? George!"

"Can't we at least stop talking about food all of the time?" he asked.

"I don't think we talk about food," Mom said. "Maybe we should. There's an elephant in the middle of the room that none of us bothers to mention. And it's made of sugar and spice and everything nice! So let's eat it, but let's not talk about it!"

. . . .

I don't like it when my parents argue. I suppose that is stating the obvious, isn't it? Who wants to listen to anyone argue? I don't remember it bothering me when I was younger, because that's kind of what we did: argue. At the dinner table we had great discussions about the issues of the day. Grandma Dottie used to laugh at us—saying it was more like a debate class than a meal. I liked it. I liked knowing more than the other kids. Other adults, too. I couldn't understand how so many people could be so deliberately ignorant. At least it seemed deliberate. When I'm an angel, I'll be able to help. I'll have abilities. They'll wash over me like the mist on the ocean my father talks about.

I don't think we talk about food a lot. No more than anyone else. I mean, food is just a part of life, right? Three meals a day at least. My dad told me once about the great potato famine. That's how his great-great-grandfather got to the United States. Most of his family had died—starved to death in Ireland. This seems to be a theme. So his great-great-whatever-grandfather got on a ship to the United States. A million or so of the Irish came to the U.S. in the 1840s, and many people thought they were vermin. Accused of all sorts of things. Great-grandpa lived in New York for a while, then drifted into Boston, where he was part of a riot or two, then ended up here, in Michigan, dirt poor, my father said, which wasn't all that bad if you actually owned the dirt.

. . . .

"Come on, darlin'," my father said. "We're going out to the Leaf for dinner."

"Dad, I'm not hungry," I said, "and I've got a paper to finish."

"You love the Leaf," he said. He put his hands on my shoulder, then quickly dropped them again. "It would really make your mother feel better."

The Leaf used to be a head shop in the hippie days, some say. Peace activists started it during the sixties. Ann Arbor was a hot bed for that kind of thing. Some say it was headquarters for the Weathermen. Mom says the men went there to talk about blowing shit up, while the women made tea and coffee for everyone.

"Yeah, it was no different in the peace movement than it was in any other place," Mom told me. "The women wanted to be a part of things, but the men ignored them, relegated them to coffee makers. Had sex with them when they felt like it. And for the most part the women went along, saying it was for a greater good. That happened before the Civil War, too. Women activists were starting to get noticed, but they were told that the struggle for the greater good meant they needed to shut up until after the slaves were freed. So they did. And women didn't get the vote in the United States until 1920."

"And the Leaf," I asked. "What about it?"

"Well, after a while the men stopped talking about blowing shit up and got jobs, and the women turned the place into a

19

tea shop. Eventually they started serving dal and rice, things like that, always with calming music—in a calming atmosphere."

Maybe that's why Mom likes it: for the "calming atmosphere." We've been going there as a family for as long as I can remember. They all know us. I used to like going there. Now I'm not so sure. I'm tired of people pointing out how skinny I am. Mom too.

Once a neighbor we don't see very often stopped us in the mall and said, "Mercy, you are getting skinny! What's your secret?"

I didn't know what to say, but my mom did.

"What a question," she said. "How do you know she isn't sick? How do you know she isn't dying of some terminal disease? If she gained weight, would you walk up to her and say, 'Mercy, you're getting fat. What's your secret?' "

The woman just stood there, her mouth open.

"Well, is she—is she sick?" The neighbor's voice trembled.

"I'm an angel," I whispered, figuring I might as well answer with the truth.

"Oh, well, I'm glad to hear it isn't serious."

The woman walked away, and my mom and I laughed. That's one thing about my mother. She is fierce in her devotion. I've never doubted she would step in front of a bullet, car, elephant, asshole, to protect me. She does it frequently. Has always done it.

"You are a wonderful, intelligent, beautiful girl," she would *often say.* "Strong, a force of Nature. Don't you ever forget it!"

And she'd kiss the top of my head, or my cheek, hand, nose. I didn't see myself—particularly—as any of those things, but it was great that she did. It was good to know that I had some-one who would watch after me. Really. To be loved that way by both of my parents is a great thing. I've always known this. I've seen other kids with their folks and wondered how they could bear to be in the world.

"Look in the mirror every day and tell yourself you're beau-tiful, you're smart, you're strong. You gotta do it yourself, sugar, cuz you can't count on anyone else to do it."

"Yes, I can," I'd tell her. "I can count on you and Dad."

"We're just fellow human beans," she'd say. "We will dis-appoint you. Probably daily."

"Beans?"

"Of course. What did you think?"

"No," I'd laugh. This was our shtick. "Human *beings*."

She'd shake her head vehemently. "Human beans. That's why we just fart around all day."

Dad and I would groan, and Mom would grin.

We have not done that in a long time.

"Mercy? Will you come?"

I looked up at my father and smiled. "'The quality of mercy is not strained.'"

"I'll take that as a yes."

. . . .

21

The car still smells like Sandy. Like damp fur.

"Do you have to take that with you everywhere?" Mom asked, turning around from the front seat. "It's worse than when you had a blankie." She was talking about my laptop.

"An apple a day keeps the doctor away," I said.

"Only if you actually eat it," Mom said.

"And it's not a 'that,' Mom," I reminded her. When I first got the laptop, after my old one gave up the ghost, Mom had asked me what I was going to call it—since I had named the last one Blue . . . because it was blue. The new laptop was white.

"I can't very well call it White," I had said. "That just sounds stupid. Or like I'm a skinhead or something."

"Hmmm," Mom had said. "Well, it could be a kind of white. Snow White. Lily White."

"Lily White. I like that. I'll call it Lily White."

Now Mom said, "Okay, do you have to bring Lily with you everywhere?"

"Lily White happens to be great company. Oh, by the way, I did a little research on the Net," I said. "There *are* angels in Judaism and Islam. And the Catholics have a whole hierarchy. Nine choirs or something like that. I didn't really understand it. But there were angels long before any of those religions. So angels are not a religious thing, per se. In case you were worried I was becoming a religious nut or something."

"That was the least of my worries," my mom muttered.

I'm feeling very nervous. Nervous. Nervous. In fact, I want to scream. I wish Sandy were here. I'd bury my face in her fur. Her wet, stinky fur. Or is it hair? Is it dog fur or dog hair? I seem to be forgetting things. I don't like it. I try not to let it scare me, though. It's like the tunnel vision I got last week. Or the week before. I was afraid I was going blind. The doctor said it was because of loss of vitamins or miner-als. He gave me an injection of something and told Mom to take me to the juice bar in the mall and make me drink. Make me drink. It was ridiculous. How can you make anyone do anything? But I was so afraid and Mom was so afraid, so I did it. I went to the juice bar and I drank. And every morning since, I've drunk the juice my mom made. Do you think that's why I'm so afraid now? I was talking about forgetting things—it feels like the tunnel vision. Then it was as though I could only see specific things. Now I can only remember specific things. But they must be the important things, right?

"Angels aren't human beings, you know," Mom said from the front seat of the car. Dad was driving.

"What do you mean?"

"Angels were never people, according to religious tra-ditions, " she said. I could tell she was trying to keep her voice matter-of-fact, but she was afraid too. "So you can't just turn into an angel."

"Maybe I always was one."

"We saw you born," Dad said. "It was the happiest day of our lives. And we've been with you every day since."

I hadn't thought of that before. They had been with me—every single day of my life.

"It's like cats and horses are different beings from each other," Mom said. "So are human beings and angels."

Human *beings*. She wasn't going to crack the joke or anything?

"Well, what do religions know?" I said. "They're just corrupt doctrines dictated by patriarchal men."

"Can't argue with you there," Mom said.

If I scream, maybe they won't make me go to the restaurant. I don't understand why I'm afraid again. Once I had this angel thing figured out, I stopped being so afraid. But now, I don't want to see anyone. I don't want anyone to see me. I've looked in the mirror. I've seen my dark eyes. The bags under them. I've seen how skinny I am. Maybe I'm wrong. Maybe I am dying. Maybe we are all dying, and there's nothing I or anyone else can do.

"Okay," Mom said. "We're all agreed that religion can be horseshit, basically. So, Mercy, my daughter, let's just assume for a moment that you are an angel. Who says angels can't eat? I've never seen a skinny angel."

"Does this mean you believe in angels, Mom?" I asked.

"I will if you start eating."

We're almost there. For some reason I keep thinking of the suffragists. Those women who went on hunger strikes so that women could get the vote. Calling them suffragettes back then was apparently an insult. Suffragists *was the more proper word. The women would protest, commit acts of vandalism, and then, once in jail, they'd go on hunger strikes. The authorities were afraid they'd die and become martyrs, so they force-fed them— and sometimes this method killed them.*

I want to scream.

"Mom, Dad. I can't breathe. Can't breathe."

Dad pulled the car over. Opened the door. I felt the cool autumn air. Dad carefully lifted me out of the car. Held me. The breeze felt like the full moon on my face. Wasn't even sure what that meant.

"It's okay, darlin'," he said. "It's okay."

"Mom. Mom. They won't do it to me like the suffragists, will they?"

"What, honey? What?" She stroked my forehead with her cool hand.

"Please." I couldn't breathe because I was sobbing.

"Does she need my inhaler?" Mom's voice was strained.

"No, no," Dad said. "Let her cry. Let her cry."

"Mom, Dad, don't let them. You won't let them force-feed me like they did those women? Shoving tubes and food down their throats and noses. You won't let them, will you?"

"Oh, no. Of course not!" Mom said. "Baby, please, can't you just eat something?"

We're home again. I'm so tired. The sun is sickly looking out my window. Covered by gray white clouds. I don't know how much longer I can sit here typing. I want to get under the covers and go to sleep.

"Did you want to call any of your friends or go see them before we leave tomorrow?" Dad asked.

"So we're really going?" I said.

"Unless there is anything you can do—like eat."

"I already called Melissa and Lou Ann," I said. "They think it's very exciting. Dramatic. But they don't really get it. Did you always know you were going to be a teacher?"

He leaned against the doorjamb and folded his arms. "No, I'm still not sure. But I was good at it. And it felt good to have people listen and to watch them learn new things. Now your mother, she was always going to be a lawyer. She was determined to bring justice to the world."

"See, that's what I feel about this, Dad," I said. "I was meant to be an angel. I'm going to do so much good."

"You don't have to do good," he said. "You just have to be Mercy. You just have to breathe. Live your life. Be an ordinary teenager."

I don't think I was ever an ordinary teenager. I had my friends, I guess. I thought about becoming a cheerleader once. For about a second. Thought about joining the drama club. For another second. Too much drama already going on around me. The eating thing began just before I started high school. I mean the not eating thing. Mom is right, though. Or was it Dad? Maybe we don't talk about food. But it's everywhere. Or is that a silly thing to say? Like saying air is everywhere. Water is everywhere. Food is everywhere. Thank goodness! That's not true in other countries. We are so lucky. So fortunate. Even though we are dying of diseases of our excesses: cancer, diabetes, heart attacks, environmental illness. No one talks about that. I see all these people taking all these medicines—my mother included—and no one questions why this is happening. Why is everyone so sick? Well, my mother questions it. She questions everything.

When Peter wasn't born, people brought food over to the house. That's a strange custom, isn't it? Or a practical one. Who wants to cook when they're grieving? My grandmother kept trying to cover up the mirrors, and my mother kept ripping the covers off.

"I don't want any of that superstitious bullshit in my house," she said. *"No disrespect intended, Ma."*

Grandma Dottie didn't say anything—she had lost her entire family, but she had never lost a child. That's what I heard her say to Grandma Rose. "God never gives us more than we can bear," Grandma Rose said as she embraced Grandma Dottie.

Grandma Dottie pulled away and said, "Oh, he most certainly does."

I remember the food from that day. Homemade apple pie. Chicken that melted off the bone. Roasted potatoes and other vegetables. Gravy. It was a feast.

I don't know why I was so hungry then. I took a plate upstairs and ate with Peter, who sat on the end of my bed. He asked me who all the people were downstairs, and I tried to tell him who everyone was.

My belly hurts. I wish Dad would go away. Not for good or anything, but just to the other room. He wants everything to be the same as it always was. Me his little girl. Mom his angry wife. He imagined I would be this smart, dedicated young woman who would get good grades and do great things—like find peace in our time. Or maybe just go to the prom with some good-looking guy who would keep his hands to himself.

I heard my mom talking to Dr. Perkins one day soon after this all started. I can hear things now. Did I say that? Like Superman. Or Superwoman, I suppose. Supergirl. Was there a Supergirl? Did she have wings? Anyway, the doctor suggested that I might want to be thin so that I could forever remain a child and never have to experience sexual feelings. I laughed out loud.

Then they started talking very softly, and I couldn't hear the rest of the conversation. I don't care about being thin. I may have at one time—for about two seconds. Maybe. I don't really remember. Everything just hurt, and I was hungry A LOT, and then I'd eat, and I could not wait to get it out of me. I couldn't wait to shit it out—I had to have it out now. So I threw up. I didn't do it for very long. Just long enough for my parents to realize I was eating them out of house and home.

1,000 young women die of anorexia every year in the United States. I've looked at sites on the net. Read some books. Most say they have no clue what causes anorexia and bulimia. Some say it has to do with chemicals and hormones. I've talked with some girls online who have it, and it is a compulsion. They can't control themselves. They just want large quantities of food—white food usually—and then they throw it back up so they don't get fat. Sometimes antidepressants help control eating disorders. I took them for a few months, and they just made me feel funny. (It didn't change my eating behavior.) Antidepressants sometimes help people with obsessive-compulsive behavior too. That's what I think anorexia nervosa is: OCD. See, I've found the cure! Now if they'd just listen to me.

I asked some of those other girls online if they were growing wings. I don't know how I put it, but I tried to be casual about it. How casual can you be when you're asking someone if she has wings? Yeah, well, that's about the reaction I got. They thought I was some kind of pervert or something, and that was the end of that conversation.

Anyway, the doctor thought I wasn't eating because of boys, so on the drive home that day my mother asked me.

"No, I'm not worried about whether boys like me or not," I told her. "This has nothing to do with boys."

"I didn't think so," she said. "Because we've talked about this."

"Yes, Mom."

At an early age they talked to me about sex, how when I got older, I would be attracted to boys—or girls—and that would be normal and natural. When I was even older, my mother explained that some people loved people of the same sex and some people loved people of the opposite sex.

"I love people of all sexes," I told her. Only I said "sixes" instead of "sexes." I was eight, maybe.

Mom laughed. "Well, that seems like a good idea."

As we drove home from the shrink, she said, "You remember we talked about girls falling in love with other girls? And that's perfectly normal. Sometimes that's the way they are for the rest of their lives, and sometimes it's not. I loved my girlfriend Jamie very much. I wanted to marry her and live out in the country with her and a bunch of kids."

"Did you have sex with her?" I asked.

She glanced at me as she drove down Washtenaw Avenue toward home. "These conversations were easier when you were little. No, we didn't have sex. It never occurred to me. I think people are more open about that stuff now."

"So you think if you were my age now, you would have had sex with Jamie?"

"Not your age," Mom said. "A bit older, I think. But yes, I think I would have—if she had been agreeable, which, come to think of it, she would not have been. Last I heard, she's married, with five kids."

"You're married too," I said. "Are you sorry?"

"No! I love your father very much," she said. "It wasn't a choice between him and Jamie, or him and any other man or woman. I just loved him."

"Why?"

"Why! You ask why? You know your father. He's adorable."

I laughed. "Yeah, but why did you love him?"

"I loved him and still do love him because he loved me absolutely. I knew when we got to our forties, he wouldn't be wandering around looking for some cute young thing. I knew if I got sick, he wouldn't be looking for someone else. I knew that he loved me, absolutely and unconditionally. And I knew he'd make a great father."

"But you only had one kid," I said. "Kind of wasted his skills."

My mom was quiet then. I had completely forgotten about Peter. I started to apologize, but I knew she wasn't mad. I knew to her it was always OK whatever I said. "Better said than dead," she'd always say—meaning that it was better to get it out in the open than to take it with you to the grave, or the grocery store. Wherever. It was just best to articulate whatever was going on. This didn't always work, of course. My father needed that time—to go to the grocery store or wherever—to think about what he wanted said. I was kind of in between. Sometimes I *blathered on and on, and sometimes I couldn't find any words to say what I was feeling.*

"I've had boyfriends," I said to Mom that day in the car. "You know, when I was younger. And I never wanted to marry any of my girlfriends. But remember Frida? Boy, her mom sure freaked out!"

We laughed. Since my parents had always encouraged me to be loving toward everyone, including my girlfriends, I was quite a demonstrative little girl. And I was always kissing and hugging on my little friends. Most of the time they'd just wipe off the kiss and carry on, but one little girl kissed me back, even on the lips a couple of times. Frida. Her parents had my parents over for a coffee conference on what they should do about this blossoming friendship. My mother said she had to sit on her hands and bite her tongue so she wouldn't say a word. "I'm sure it would be all right for your child to grow up to be a lesbos," the mother said, "since you're in the arts—teaching at the university and everything, and you being an environmental lawyer. That does kind of spell d-y-k-e, doesn't it? But Frida is a refined child of the highest breeding." My mom laughed, Dad said, but he told the woman—and man—that they were a couple of inbred little bigots and he and Mom didn't want their little lesbos daughter playing with their daughter anyway.

Of course, none of this had any influence on Frida and me. We continued playing at school. She continued kissing me, until one day she was chewing cinnamon gum when she kissed me on the mouth, and the smell grossed me out and I never let her do it again. Mom and Dad didn't tell me the story of Frida's parents until just a couple of years ago. I thought it was quite funny. Frida did not grow up to become the refined young lady her parents were hoping for—although boys are now more to her liking than girls. She has a new one every other day, it seems. Sometimes she winks at me in the school hallways, and I wonder what is going on in her life. In her brain.

Some boy called me and another girl "lesbos" once. In junior high. I went home and asked my mother what it meant.

"It means that boy was a little asshole," she said.

"No, really, what is a lesbos?"

"I told you some women fall in love with women and some women fall in love with men."

I nodded. "Yes."

"The women who fall in love with women are called lesbians. The word comes from Lesbos, which is a Greek island. In the olden days women lived in communities there and had much more freedom than they probably had in other parts of Greece, which was a very patriarchal society."

By that age, I knew what Mom meant when she said "patriarchal." "It's not men against women or women hating men, it's about a system which makes slaves of us all. Which works to pit us against one another. It's a system."

"This system sounds like a very bad person," I said when she first told me about the patriarchy.

"It's not a person," she said. "It's a way of being in the world."

"Like human beans?"

She laughed and hugged me. "I'll explain it when you're older."

"I know," I said. "It's like the dogs Charlie and Brutus next door. Charlie is always so mean to Brutus, and Brutus crouches down and tries to be nice to Charlie so that he won't get beat up so much. But when Charlie is gone, Brutus rips up their toys, he spills their water, eats all their food. Then Charlie and the Devlins are pissed at him. If Charlie wouldn't treat Brutus so bad, he probably wouldn't do all those things. It's a bad system."

"You got it, my daughter."

But I'm getting you lost. I'm telling you too many things. I'm remembering all these things, and they're coming all at once, as though I have to put them down before I forget them. But I remember looking up Lesbos when I was older and finding out about the poet Sappho. Some sources said the Amazons lived on Lesbos. The Amazons! Can you imagine! What would that be like, knowing your whole life that you were important, strong, capable, and that you could take care of yourself? Not only that, but that the culture supported you in being yourself. I see how my mother struggles every day in a system that doesn't seem to support her. She is always the one pointing out something is wrong.

"I'm a fucking Cassandra in a world where everyone already has their fingers in their ears," she would often say. "I'm sorry, sweetie. I sound so bitter, don't I? If I wanted happy endings, I shouldn't have gone into environmental law, eh?"

When I was little, the three of us would lie on my bedroom

floor with my plastic horses and several small dolls, and we would play Amazons. The father and mother would teach the girl to ride horses, write poetry, do archery, run marathons, govern wisely, and the girl would do all these things with skill—although it wasn't always easy. I was not always the girl, however. I often made my father or mother be the child, so I could be the parent.

In junior high I had a mythology class, and the teacher started talking about the Amazons, saying they cut off one breast so they would be better archers and they killed all their male children. I raised my hand and said, "Excuse me, but they didn't cut off their breasts. For one thing, ouch, and for another thing, if they had actually done anything so stupid, there would have been a lot of scar tissue which would have made them worse archers, not better ones. And another thing, have you ever birthed a child? No mother is going to kill her baby boy just because it's a baby boy." Of course, I didn't know then about the little Chinese girls who were often left out on hillsides to die, but that's another story. Anyway, I could see the teacher was not happy with me.

"Mercy, it's a myth. Someone made up the story of the Amazons, so they can say whatever they want about them."

I shook my head. "If by 'myth' you mean they didn't exist, I'm afraid you're wrong. They were real."

I was sent to detention for being disrespectful. When I got home that afternoon, my mom and dad asked how my day went.

"I'm a fucking Cassandra in a world where everyone already has their fingers in their ears," I said. "If I wanted happy endings, I shouldn't have gone into junior high, eh?"

My mom laughed so hard she nearly wet her pants.

So where is all this going? I don't know. To show you that I am really an angel. I'm not crazy. I didn't have a screwed-up childhood. I am on my way to where I need to be going.

"Darlin', it's too cold out here for you," my father said as he put his coat around me.

I was standing under the huge old oak in our backyard, at Sandy's grave. I was also shivering uncontrollably.

"Come on," he said.

I think it was starting to rain.

"I wanted to see if Sandy was out here," I said. "You know, on a tree limb or something, the way Peter was when he died."

My father was practically carrying me inside the house.

"What do you mean?" he asked when we were in the foyer.

I followed him into the kitchen and stood on the heat register to get warm.

"Peter used to sit at the end of my bed," I said. "For a couple of years."

"What did he say?"

I shrugged. "We just talked," I said. "I told him about my day."

"You never said."

"I thought it would hurt your feelings," I said, "or you'd think I was crazy. But since you already think I'm crazy . . ."

"I don't think you are crazy," he said. "Neither does your mother. I don't think you have any control over this eating thing. That's why we're sending you to the hospital. They have medications that will help you."

"Can we go see Grandma and Grandpa before we go?"

"They're up north visiting Uncle Bruce and Aunt Em," Dad said. "You'll see them soon."

"How do you know? The average stay at Mercywood is fifty days!"

"Oh, well, they told us you'd probably be there two weeks, and we'd come and work with you."

"I want to see Grandma and Grandpa."

"We could fly them out to New Mexico," he said.

"No! I don't want them to know about this," I said. "You've told them? I do not have an eating disorder, Dad."

I got along with Grandma Dottie better than Grandma and Grandpa O'Connor. I had to be careful about what I said around them. It was easy to send them into the cornfield. That's what we used to call it. My cousins and me. Did you ever see that old Twilight Zone *episode where this bad-seed kid would send people he didn't like into the cornfield—where something hideous apparently happened to them? My cousins Theresa and Jeffrey and I would go out into my grandparents' cornfields and try to figure out what would be so horrible about being in the cornfield. Some kind of metaphor, we figured, although I don't think we* ever used that word before we had freshman English. Then one day we saw Grandma and Grandpa in the cornfield, and they were kind of staring into space, quiet, looking all blank slate and everything—like they did whenever us kids (or my mom) starting talking about something they didn't want to talk about. The three of us just started laughing, all thinking of that stupid black-and-white episode of The Twilight Zone.

What's strange is that my mom knew exactly what was going on. One day when we were at their house, my grandparents kind of spaced out, went "cornfield," and Jeffrey, Theresa, and I started laughing and doing the theme from The Twilight Zone. My mom took the newspaper she was reading and playfully swatted me on the bottom.

"Be thankful I don't believe in beating children," she called as the three of us ran away laughing, "unless they really need it."

Later she said she didn't like seeing me be disrespectful to my grandparents.

"Isn't it disrespectful of them to just go away like that in the middle of a conversation?" I asked.

"They don't mean it as a sign of disrespect," my mother said. "They're trying to avoid conflict. For them, having conflict is a sign of disrespect."

"How can you avoid conflict?" I asked. "Talk about the weather all the time?"

"As long as you don't bring up global warming, yes," she said.

But sometimes it was comforting to be with my grandparents.

We did the same things every time I visited. They talked about the same things. Or didn't talk. Sometimes when I was with them, we didn't say a word for what seemed like hours. After Peter wasn't born, I stayed with them for a few days or weeks. I would help Grandma get dinner ready while Grandpa sat at the kitchen table drinking coffee and reading the newspaper. Something so comforting about the way he rustled and then turned the pages of the paper, his sighs, the sound of Grandma's knife chopping through the vegetables. Every once in a while Grandma would look down at me and smile or Grandpa would look over his paper at me and wink. We all breathed together in the silence. It was perfect.

I never knew I longed for that kind of silence until I had it.

I don't think Grandma and Grandpa understood Mom, but they loved her all the same. And she them. Whenever any of Mom's girlfriends started complaining about their in-laws, Mom would say, "Mine are great. Wouldn't trade them for anybody!" Once she looked over at me and winked just like Grandpa did and whispered, "A little fond of the cornfield, but so what? I'm a little fond of the bottle."

Which was a joke, because my mother didn't drink. Neither of my parents do. So you see? My immediate and extended family are all upright, loving citizens. I was never misused or abused. I was treated with respect at nearly every turn.

Why am I telling you all this? It's my parents I need to convince. My father is making us breakfast.

. . . .

"It's like having diabetes," my father said. "You would need to get treatment for that, and you need to get treatment for this."

I heard my mother come down the stairs but didn't see her yet.

"I was just looking at a site on the Web called Fathers for something," I said. "I don't remember what. And they were saying that the problem of anorexia and bulimia was greatly exaggerated by the feminists. That really we should be looking at much bigger problems."

I was blathering. Panic talking.

"Exaggerated? What kind of site was this? Nancy, did you hear that? We shouldn't be worrying about this eating disorder because the *feminists* have exaggerated it."

"Oh, yeah." My mother came into the kitchen. She looked tired. Didn't sleep. "I've seen them. It's an antiabortion site. They're against anything they call feminist. Strange group of people."

"I went on an antiabortion site once by accident," I said. "I typed in the site I wanted, but I forgot the period, and it took me to this antiabortion site. There were photographs. It was horrible." I put my hand over my eyes. I didn't want to remember it.

"Yes, they're against abortion, but they're not against picking up the pieces and taking photographs of them," Mom said. "I'm sorry you had to see that. Do you want me to try putting some filters on your computer?"

I shook my head.

"No one said making those kinds of decisions wasn't tough," Mom said. "If someone doesn't believe in abortion, then she shouldn't have one."

"Did you ever have an abortion?" I asked.

My mother shook her head. "No, they weren't legal until I was eighteen. I remember walking through the mall near our house, and they had these huge blown-up photographs of aborted fetuses. Before the ruling. It was disgusting. They didn't have any blown-up photographs of the women who died because of botched abortions. Why are we talking about this now? Mercy, did you pack last night? Do you need help? We need to be at the airport by eleven o'clock to get through all the screening processes. Wear tennis shoes—no metal in your tennis shoes. Might get us through more quickly."

"Are you going to lecture each and every airport and airplane employee about our civil rights and how they've been eroded by all the fearmongers?" my father asked.

"Evil prevails where good people do nothing," my mother said.

"It's okay with me," I said. "She can lecture them all. The Patriot Act sucks. You go, Mom."

Mom raised an eyebrow, then glanced at Dad.

"I think I'm being played here, my husband," she said. "I will be the model of the docile run-with-the-herd American. We will not miss our flight."

The doorbell rang. We all heard Aunt Lenny's voice.

"Hello, hello, dear ones. Sister Sue is here!"

Aunt Lenny—Mom's older sister—sashayed into the kitchen. "Hello, sugar." She gave Mom a kiss on the cheek. "Hi, sailor." Another kiss for Dad. "Hello, angel!" She embraced me heartily.

When she let me go, I said, "See, Aunt Lenny knows!"

My mother rolled her eyes.

"Stay to breakfast?" Dad asked as he cracked eggs into a bowl.

"Sure, I'm starving!"

Aunt Lenny took off her sunglasses and swung them around while she gazed at me.

"You wanna make a break for it?" she asked. Her real name is Marlene, but Mom and Uncle Maxwell shortened it to Lenny when they were kids.

"Yes!"

She grabbed me, and we ran into the living room and plopped down on the couch.

"You okay?" she asked.

"No," I said. "I don't want to go. I'm not crazy, Aunt Lenny. I don't have an eating disorder. I did for a while, but then it all became clear to me. I don't need to eat."

"Well, you go to this place, and they'll do all kinds of tests on you," Aunt Lenny said. "If you're healthy, they'll send you home. If you need some nutritional support, they'll help you with that."

"I guess."

"Here, I brought you a present," she said. She dug in her purse, pulled out a small box, and handed it to me.

I opened it. Inside a wooden *mala* was curled up like a snake. On the inside of the cover of the box was a picture of the goddess Tara.

"Thanks, Aunt Lenny," I said.

"Do you remember the mantra?"

I smiled. "Wow. It's been so many years."

Aunt Lenny's spirituality was somewhat eclectic. When I was a little girl, I sometimes had trouble settling down. I would get so wound up that I would spin around in circles—as if trying to unwind, literally. Then Aunt Lenny figured out how to calm me. We would go into the closet in my room and close the door. We'd sit in the dark, cross-legged—in the lotus position—and chant.

"Close your eyes and breathe," Aunt Lenny said now—in real time and in my memory.

I did as she said, just as I had when I was a little girl. I held the new *mala* between my thumb and forefinger.

"You are standing on the shores of a beautiful lake. Across the lake, on the opposite bank, you see a woman—she's lovely, light radiates from her. She might even be a teenager, laughing and happy. As you chant, she gets into a small boat and rows to you. As she comes nearer, joy fills your being. *Om Tara tu tare ture soha.*"

We chanted together until we had gone all around the *mala*: 108 beads.

"You know," Aunt Lenny said. "Tara is a bodhisattva. She could have gone on, left this wheel of suffering, but she decided to stay on Earth until all people had achieved enlightenment. It is said that Tara is 'she who hears the cries of the world.' You just whisper her name, or her mantra, and she'll help you out."

"I wonder if people thought she was crazy," I said.

"No doubt," Aunt Lenny said. She squeezed my arm. "You'll be all right, honey. Just hang in there. Your mom and dad are doing what they think will help."

"I know."

"Now, let's go eat some breakfast," she said. "I'll eat like a horse, and you can just push your food around on the plate and pretend."

I did eat a bit of breakfast. When I put the fork in my mouth— the fork that had some egg on it—the entire room changed. Everyone suddenly started talking, even laughing. A bit of hysteria, it seemed. I couldn't taste the egg.

Did I say? My wings have been itching. I could hardly sleep last night they itched so much.

We're in the air now. At the airport my mother did not preach to anyone about anything. In fact, she barely said a word, just kept straightening things: my hair, my sweater, my jacket, Dad's hair, Dad's jacket. We're above the clouds. Sunshine. I sit by the window. The stewardess brought us something to eat, but no one wanted anything. Aunt Lenny drove us to the airport. Mom doesn't like to fly—which makes it even more amazing that she was so quiet.

In the storybooks, heaven often looks like this. Golden. Above the clouds. Why is that? My mother is reading a book about angels.

"You know, Mom, I can tell you what you need to know about angels," I said. "You can just ask."

She nodded and looked up from the book. "The writer compared angels to bodhisattvas."

"Aunt Lenny said the same thing this morning," I said. "You two in cahoots?"

"Did she? No, we're not in cahoots. This writer also says that angels were originally mostly female. Then Christianity got a hold of them and turned them into men."

"That's just politics, Mom. It doesn't have anything to do with reality."

"What do you mean?"

"Just because the culture believed angels were female and then said they were male doesn't make them male—or female. It doesn't have anything to do with what is true."

"You have always been so old, my daughter," Mom said. "An old soul."

"The better to be an angel, don't you think?"

My mom made a face.

"Mom, do you think talking to people about things really changes their minds?" I asked. "You know, talking about pollution, our civil rights, war, peace, stuff like that. You say 'Evil prevails where good people do nothing.'"

She shook her head. "I don't really think it does any good."

"But you're always arguing with people," I said. "Why do you do it if you don't believe in it?"

"I used to believe in discourse, discussion. People used to talk to one another and listen, change their minds. I don't see that happening so much anymore. It's just a war of words, nobody listening—everyone talking. Including me. Plus I think everyone is on information overload. They don't know what to do about all the horrible things they hear about."

"But you keep doing it."

"For me, I don't want things to sneak up on me," she said. "You know? I want to know what's coming, as much as I can know. My mother's family was surprised by the Holocaust. My dad, too, even though he wasn't in the camps. They just couldn't believe what was happening, and I think that kept them from acting. Some people believed it was happening—knew it was coming—and they got away. I'm not blaming them. I don't mean that at all. I mean, who could believe such a thing was possible? But I keep myself informed. So that I know *anything* is possible."

"Even good things?"

"I don't know, honey," she said. "I just don't know."

Dad slept next to my mother. I smiled.

"He can sleep anywhere," she said. "Mercy, I won't force you to go into the hospital. I don't want you to feel forced."

"'The quality of mercy is not strained'?" I said.

My mother looked at me. "Just let them check you out. If everything is fine, then come home."

"'It droppeth as the gentle rain from heaven,'" I whispered as I gazed out the window, "'upon the place beneath.'"

I think I'd like to stay up here forever. Wouldn't that be something? Just to float above it all. All the chaos and turmoil is below. Up here it's just wind. And clouds. Sprites, blue jets, elves. Have you heard of them? "Jets" are these huge columns of energy that extend up to 40 miles above a thunderstorm. Some people describe them as looking like giant carrots and trees. Then there are the "sprites"—they're bursts of lightning above thunderclouds. I think those are the ones that look like huge jellyfish. Elves, too. Gigantic, all of them. The jets go right out into outer space. I love looking at the photos on the internet. They do seem whimsical, something more than just lightning or electrical activity—but then, aren't we humans basically electrical activity? Anyway, they are beautiful—like dancing color. Light. Goddesses. Something that makes me think maybe there is something besides just us. Maybe they're angels—or bodhisattvas, devas, spirits, whatever.

I wish I could see them. But we are over land, and the sprites, jets, and elves seem to occur only over water. Why do you think that would be? Are they in love with the ocean, sea, lake? A manifestation of an exchange between water and clouds—their mating creates these gorgeous, colorful dancers of electricity?

My mom leans against my father.

I hope that I am doing the right thing. I was so certain. Now I'm not sure. I haven't seen the wings in days, even though I can feel them itching. I suppose today my wings are the wings of this jet, taking us to Albuquerque. I certainly haven't gotten any signs from anything Divine, telling me I'm on the right track. The word angel *means "messenger." What kind of messenger am I? Who knows? The word* mercy *has the same root in common with* Mercury, *that ol' hermaphrodite god who hung out with the goddess. He was a messenger god too. By "too" I don't mean I'm a messenger god. I just mean we might both be messengers.*

I'm babbling again, aren't I? Fear does that. And joy, I suppose. But I don't remember joy.

Do you?

An ant is crawling on Lily White's screen. How do you suppose it got here, on this plane? I hope it'll stay safe. Although I don't know how. I think if ants lose the scent of the trail, they just go around in circles until they die because they don't know how to get home again. I wonder if that happens to people, too. They lose the scent—or the sense—of home, so they wander around in circles, not knowing how to get back on the path, until they die. How would we get back home without this airplane? I haven't walked the land. I didn't leave my scent. No one from my family has left theirs. If it weren't for this technology, I would never make it back, would I? If I were outside this airplane, would I leave my scent upon these clouds? This sky?

Maybe the blue jets, sprites, and elves are dancing their way along a sky trail, following the scent of their tribe, lighting up the sky with the joy of a being who knows the way home.

The plane lands heavy, it seems, with a bounce or a trip. Mom grabs Dad's hand. I feel discombobulated, as Grandma Rose would say. As if I'm suddenly heavy too, and I'm not sure I like being Earthbound again. For some reason I think of Prometheus, chained to a mountain getting his liver eaten every day because he gave fire and reason to people. Until Hercules released him. How that must have felt after nearly forever! Prometheus Unbound. This makes me think of Percy Shelley, who wrote a play named Prometheus Unbound *after his wife Mary Shelley wrote* Frankenstein, or The Modern Prometheus. *We're in the rental car now. Driving toward. Driving toward. Mary Shelley's mother died giving birth to her. Do you think that's why she wrote a book about a creature created but not birthed? She was only a few years older than I am now when she wrote Frankie. Most of her babies died. Her mother was Mary Wollstonecraft: the woman who wrote* A Vindication of the Rights of Woman. *Mom read that to me when I was younger. That and the declaration of women's rights at Seneca Falls. I have part of that memorized, still. I think.*

The sky is so blue. It's a blue like no other blue. Have you ever seen Georgia O'Keeffe's paintings? I mean in real life. True life. She knew the color. It's not the bluest blue. Or the lightest blue. Or the most turquoise blue. It's the luckiest blue. Yeah, that's it. Like you are so lucky you get to see this blue. People paint their doors blue here, just to have that kind of luck I bet.

"We hold these truths to be self-evident, that all men and women are created equal." In 1848 the women at Seneca Falls wrote this. Before the Civil War. Mary's mom wrote Vindication in the 1700s. 1791? Frankenstein was in 1818, I think, I think.

We travel down Highway 40, past Santa Fe. I go in and out of sleep. Dreaming time.

A dog is running beside the car. Looks just like Sandy. Blondish. I guess that's why we called her Sandy. And a boy is waving to me from an adobe house. He looks like Peter. I return the wave and blink. No Sandy. No Peter.

We're going too fast.

"Dad, I'm going to be sick."

I don't know if I can do this. Do this. Do this. It'll make my parents feel better. Just stay for a while. Can't believe I threw up. Yuck. Reminds me of when I was bingeing and purging. It's hard to believe I ever did that on purpose. Now I'm sitting in the front seat. The hills wobble on either side of me, looking like a Georgia O'Keeffe painting. Lucky blue sky. Red rock hills, mixed with cream, dotted with pear-shaped bits of green. Reminding me of a fake landscape created for someone's toy train set. Do you know what I mean?

What I mean.

What I mean.

Take a deep breath. Breathe. Breathe.

Om Tara tu tare ture soha.

I'm in a boat, rowing to She Who Hears the Cries of the World.

In a boat.

Cries of the world.

Seasick.

A sign.

Literally.

MERCYWOOD.

Angels on either side of the sign.

Bad sign. Bad sign.

"Are they religious?" I ask.

"No, no," Mom says.

Is the road paved? I can't concentrate.

Om Tara tu tare ture soha.

The beads move quickly through my fingers.

"Isn't it beautiful?" Dad says.

For a moment, I feel fuzzy. Like I'm flying. I hear the fluttering of wings.

And I know

I am most certain

That the wings I hear are my own.

part two

A woman who looked and smelled like a peach came out of a long, one-story building that settled into the hillside like something Frank Lloyd Wright created. Part of the landscape. I wanted to touch the peach fuzz on the woman's cheek.

"Judith Gardner," the woman said, holding out her hand to me. I shook it. Firm, matter-of-fact. "I'm the director of Mercywood and one of the counselors."

She looked more like a ranch hand than a therapist. Comparing her with Dr. Perkins. Dr. Perkins was soft, in a nice way. Judith Gardner was peachy from the sun, her jeans faded from time and work. The sunshine made everything sharper here—in focus. Different from Michigan sun.

Judith Gardner shook hands with Mom and Dad. In

the near distance, a group of girls and women sat in a circle. They shimmered, like heat mirages. None of them had wings.

"That will be you in a few days," Judith Gardner said.

I looked at Judith and then at the group again.

Was I going to begin to disappear too?

After we first arrived, everything seemed to blur away. Like a dream. Or like being on stage. Judith Gardner took us inside. Cool. Calming, I suppose. Colors, design, all that: I haven't a clue. We followed her somewhere, sat in an office disguised as a living room but it was an office, where Judith talked and Mom and Dad asked questions. At one point, she asked me if I was checking myself in, and I nodded. My mouth was so dry. She gave me a couple sheets of paper with a schedule on them—one to my parents, too. I tried to read it but my eyes couldn't scan it, or something. Regiment. So much regimen.

"Stability helps our clients with eating disorders," Judith said, smiling.

"Isn't that redundant? Clients with *eating disorders*. Isn't this a hospital for people with eating disorders?"

Oops. I said that out loud.

"We're a treatment center, Mercy," Judith said. "Not a hospital."

"What's the difference?"

"The white coats," Judith said. She smiled.

A beat or two later we laughed. So a sense of humor.

"We don't allow Internet here," Judith said. She was looking at Lily White. "Too many pro-ana sites."

"Pro-ana?" my mother asked.

"Pro-anorexia," Judith said. "Anorexics and bulimics get online to find out from one another how to lose weight, how to fool their parents and friends, how to exercise."

"You're kidding?" Dad looked over at me. "Did you know about these?"

I nodded. "Sure, but I wasn't interested. And I am still not interested. Do you know why? Because I do *not* have an eating disorder."

"It's more of a journal," Mom said. "Her computer. I see you have journaling on the schedule."

"That's true," Judith said, "and some of the girls do have their laptops with them for that. You can't get wireless Internet out here anyway, so it should be all right."

Mom squeezed my hand. She had maneuvered that smoothly.

"I should let you know we lock all the bathrooms," Judith said, "so there is no chance for bingeing and purging."

At least not in the bathrooms.

None of this felt angelic. It just felt medical. Hospital-like, contaminated with sickness.

And barf.

At some point a girl came into the living room slash office.

"Bluebird will take you to your room," Judith said. "I have a few things to go over with your parents."

I followed Bluebird away from the a-dults. She did not seem too thin.

"Bluebird? That's your name? How cool."

She came up close to me. "It's really Ana, but J.G. won't let me use it. She figured it was code for *anorexia*. Look at me. I've gained ten pounds. That's what 'recovery' will do for you!" She held up the first two fingers of each hand and stroked the air when she said "recovery."

Another girl appeared from somewhere and walked with us.

"Snapshot, this is Mercy," Bluebird said. "Mercy, Snapshot."

"Do you all have nicknames?"

"Sure," Snapshot said. "I like your name. Mercy. Mercywood. Are you our new savior? Has she met Suzy-Q yet?"

"No, asshole, that's where I'm taking her," Bluebird said matter-of-factly. I wondered how old she was. Eighteen? Twelve? Brown hair cut real short. And Snapshot. Skinny (of course). Stringy blond hair.

"Three ribs showing," Snapshot said.

"Pardon me?" I asked.

"I have three ribs showing," she said, twirling around. "Ain't it grand?"

"Shhhh. One of the counselors hears you and we're all up shit's creek without a barf bag."

Snapshot giggled. I smiled.

We stopped at a closed blue door. Reminded me of a hotel.

"Only twenty-two of us here," Bluebird said.

"Anorexia ain't what it used to be," Snapshot said.

"Suzy-Q is the skinniest."

"Our queen!"

The door suddenly opened. A tall, very thin woman stood where the door had just been.

"I still reign," Suzy-Q said, looking me up and down. "Yay." It was more of a sigh than a cheer. "You're bunking with me, kid."

I walked into the small room, decorated Southwestern style, earth tones, subdued lighting, Mexican blankets on the bed.

"Nauseating, isn't it? Just think of it next time you need to purge, and it'll help you out." She slowly sat on the bed closest to the window. She moved like an old woman.

Bluebird and Snapshot hung on the door and didn't come into the room.

"Suzy-Q is a model," Bluebird said. "She knows all the tricks."

I cleared my throat. "Don't any of you want to get better?"

Suzy-Q laughed. "I'm only here because my agent wouldn't book any more work for me until I agreed to come. So here I am. I never promised anything else. Just to come here. Why? Do you want to get better?"

"I'm not sick," I said. "I don't have an eating disorder."

"Right on, girl," Snapshot said.

"Mercy, mercy. Got a nickname?" Suzy-Q asked.

I shook my head.

"I hear we've got a newbie," another girl said as she came to stand between Bluebird and Snapshot.

"This is Mia," Snapshot said.

"No nickname?" I sat on my bed. I bounced a bit. Seemed comfy enough. The other girls—and woman—watched me.

"Doesn't that hurt?" Bluebird asked.

"No, why should it?"

They looked at one another and shrugged.

"Mia is her nickname, and Judith Gardner can't do anything about it because it's her real name," Snapshot said. She raised her hand, and Mia slapped it.

"I don't understand," I said.

"Mia—buli*mia*," Suzy-Q said. "Now, how about you? Let's think of a name for her. Tell us about yourself."

I shrugged. Why not?

"I had an eating disorder after my dog died and my

grandma moved away and I started high school," I said. "But it went away."

"But you're still skinny," Mia said.

"I still don't eat," I said, "because I'm an angel and I don't need to eat."

That certainly stopped the conversation. I think they were all holding their breath.

"I thought I heard the rustling of wings when you came into the room," Suzy-Q said, "but I gotta tell ya, honey, I can't *see* a thing. You better work on that."

The girls all laughed. I couldn't tell whether they were making fun of me or laughing with me.

"Well, I wrote in Lily White that my name is Mercy, or The Angel Mercy. If you take the first letter of those three words, then I'm Tam."

"Tam. Tammy! Yes, that's *perfect,*" Suzy-Q said. "They'll never know what it means."

"What does Suzy-Q mean?"

The model shrugged her barely shoulders. "I just like the song."

The four of them began singing "Suzie Q" and dancing around the room. Only each of them was singing her own verse, her own lines. After a few moments they all stopped, seemingly exhausted.

"Fuck me," Suzy-Q said, sitting on the bed again.

I think I heard her wheezing.

My stomach started to hurt. I DID NOT BELONG HERE.

I want to go home. Go home. Go home.

Mom and Dad stayed for dinner. They helped me put my clothes away first. Suzy-Q left us alone. The room smelled peculiar. I couldn't place it. Laxatives? Puke? Sickness?

I started to cry. Mom and Dad hugged me.

"I don't want to be an angel," I said. "I just want to be a girl. I don't feel like I have control over anything."

I wanted to scream. To run from the reality of everything. Whatever that was.

"We know, sugar," Mom whispered. "We'll just be a few miles away. You can call anytime."

"But it says on my schedule that I can only call between four thirty and ten P.M."

"If you really need to talk to us, you find someone and tell them it's an emergency," Dad said.

I nodded. Panic dulled everything again except my fear.

The girls—and women—stood in line for their meds before dinner. Reminded me of *One Flew over the Cuckoo's Nest.* Except no one wore a white uniform. I hoped I wasn't McMurphy. Didn't want to get my brains fried.

"Do they do electric shock here?" I asked.

We sat at a wooden table made to look like a regular kitchen table, not something from a hospital cafeteria. But that was what it was.

Be all you can be.

"Of course not," Mom said. "This place is recommended by all the experts in the field."

"Experts in the field of angelology?" I asked.

"Eating disorders," Dad said, as if I really needed an answer.

The girls I had met earlier sat at the other tables, purposely leaving the three of us alone, I guessed. Someone brought us plates. Tonight I could eat—or not eat—whatever I wanted. Judith had said they would try not to give me any "trigger" foods—foods that normally freak out anorexics and the like. No mashed potatoes. Instead a green salad and steamed fish. Rice. I ate little bites of each.

"You seem to be eating better," Mom said.

Because I was actually eating.

I nodded. I couldn't feel anything but the horrible knot in my stomach. Had I suddenly grown a stomach tumor in the last couple of hours? I felt like I couldn't breathe.

"Isn't there something else we could do?" I whispered, leaning down so Mom and Dad could hear me. I didn't look at the other girls to see if they were eating. It seemed so quiet. Huge picture windows looked out at the desert. The sun was setting, turning the red rock rose-colored, the evergreens black. A blond dog ran along the ridge of a hill.

"Look," I said. "I keep seeing Sandy."

Mom and Dad followed my gaze.

"It's a coyote, sugar," Dad said. "The trickster. Perhaps he—or she—is welcoming you to the desert."

"You think?" I asked.

"Sure, sure," Mom said. I knew she didn't mean it.

"The girls I met," I whispered, "they aren't trying to get better."

"What do you mean?" Mom asked.

"They're trying to stay skinny."

Mom looked alarmed—you know, the way mothers do, pretending it's nothing when you know they are screaming inside.

Mom glanced at Dad. He shrugged. Lotta help there, Dad.

"Well, just don't pay any attention to them," Mom said.

"What if they're all like that?" I said. "It'll be like prison. Some nice guy goes into prison and comes out a criminal because he's surrounded by criminals. I'm coming here like that nice guy, and I'm surrounded by girls with eating disorders, so I'll come out with an eating disorder."

My parents looked at me. Oh, I forgot. They already thought I had an eating disorder.

"Mom, Mom! Do you remember when I was a kid and wouldn't go to camp? Do you remember? Did I ever tell you why? 'Cause Grandma Dottie had been in a concentration camp. And I was afraid you were sending me to the same kind of camp. And I was so afraid. That I'd starve to death. That people would drop dead around me. That they'd figure out I was part Jewish. Or something. Mom, Mom. This feels like the same thing. *Mom.* Help me."

"No, no, no, sugar. This isn't the same. You're not going to starve here. They're going to help you get better. It's not a camp. It's not any kind of camp. Sugar, sugar. It's okay."

"That's what your grandma told Grandma Dottie when they were in the cattle cars, Mom. Mom. Didn't she tell you? 'It'll be all right. They wouldn't hurt us. You're just a girl. I'm just a woman. They won't hurt us. It'll be like a vacation, out in the country. Don't worry, my daughter.' Just like you, Mom. She called her 'my daughter,' just like you. Only nothing was all right."

My mother opened her mouth, but no words came out.

I am going to scream. Vomit. Throw it all up. I cannot bear any of it. How did I get here? When did it start? Why did I think I was an angel? I wasn't good. I wasn't sweet.

Sugar. Sugar. Honey. Honey.

"I can't be nice, Mom. I can't. Only the good die young. I don't want to be nice."

"You don't need to be. It is not required. Just breathe, Mercy. Breathe."

"You're a fine one to talk," I said. "Why don't *you* just fucking well breathe!"

I don't talk this way. Ever. Have never had any desire to.

Have I risen my voice? Is that the right thing to say? Have I risen from the dead? Dying?

I can't see or hear or anything. Feel my mother's hand on one arm, my father's hand on the other arm. I'm going to scream.

Don't fucking touch me.

Don't leave me.

Don't leave me.

"Mercy will do great here."

I look up and Suzy-Q is standing there, tall and thin, moving slightly, as if from a breeze. She is a willow, I decide. A willow that has forgotten to eat. Her hand rests on my shoulder. I look to see, but it is not there. Her arms are at her sides, her fingers twitching slightly.

"We'll take care of her," Suzy-Q said. "After dinner we do processing. Would you like to come sit with us?"

She is all sweetness and light.

Judith comes and takes my parents away for a while.

I see too many skinny girls. A woman—Tracy (they all have such Anglo-Saxon names)—leads the discussion.

"I didn't feel anything," one of the girls says.

"I wanted to be sick, but I ate it anyway." Someone else.

"It had a strange texture. Like dog poop." Someone.

"How would you know?" Else.

"But how did you feel?"

"Contaminated."

Suzy-Q rolls her eyes again and again, until I think for sure they just roll around the room. Bluebird and Snapshot doodle with their fingers in the salt on the table.

FUK, they draw.

I watch the mouths of the girls move. I am looking at a Day of the Dead tableau, clothed skeletons yakking away.

Suzy-Q leans closer to me.

"Don't worry, love. It'll only get worse. Did you ever see those old Tammy movies? With Debbie Reynolds, I think."

I shake my head. Someone is describing what the food felt like going down her throat. "It's like it's talking to me. 'You're gonna get fat, you're gonna get fat.'"

"Tammy and the Bachelor. Tammy and the Doctor. *Titles* like that. Well, this can be your Tammy and the Disordered."

I laugh.

"Ahhh, I heard it again."

"What?"

"The rustling of your wings, Tammy dear."

Mom and Dad left just before lights out. I watched them drive away. The porch light went out, and I stood in total darkness. A coyote—I guess—howled in the distance. Only it sounded more like it was crying than howling.

"Sweet dreams," Suzy-Q said when I got into bed.

We slept with the door closed. I fell to sleep with Aunt Lenny's *mala* wrapped around my wrist, reciting, "*Om Tara tu tare.*" Was this what it was like to be in a cage? In the night I got up to open the window, sucked on the cool air, and noticed Suzy-Q wasn't in bed. I heard a noise coming from the closet. I walked over to it and started to open the door. Instead, I knocked.

"You okay?"

The door opened. I couldn't see Suzy-Q, but I knew she was there.

"Shhh. You can exercise in here and no one can hear you. Coming to this place has really interrupted my exercise schedule. You want to join me?" The darkness was speaking to me.

"Uh, no. Maybe another time."

"Okay." The door shut again.

I went back to bed. I wasn't able to sleep until Suzy-Q came back to bed.

I awakened to sobbing. I thought. But when I sat up, I heard nothing except people walking in the hall, whispering.

"The shower room is open," Suzy-Q said as she pulled on a pair of slacks. Her legs were like . . .

bones. "But Sarge watches everything. No purging."

"I-I think I'm clean enough," I said.

"Suit yourself. Gotta go weigh in. Wear your heaviest clothes."

Suzy-Q pulled on another pair of slacks and two sweatshirts. "I'm of two minds," she said. "I don't like it when the scales say I weigh more, but they've already got me on enough drugs and food. I need to at least look like I'm gaining weight. You coming?"

"Go ahead."

I quickly pulled on a pair of jeans and a shirt. Then I went to the bathroom. A woman stood outside the door.

"Hello, Mercy," she said. "I'm Shelley." Like Mary Shelley? Was I her Frankenstein?

"I just have to pee," I said. "And splash my face."

She nodded. I went inside. It looked and smelled like our high school locker room. I went into one of the stalls and peed. I heard the door open and close. When I came out, Shelley was washing her hands. I did the same.

"There are extra towels and washcloths over there," she said, nodding toward a closet. I went over and grabbed a washcloth and quickly washed my face.

How creepy to be watched like this.

"I don't purge," I said, and left the bathroom.

I followed a couple of girls down the hallway to a room next to the cafeteria slash dining room. My schedule said this was the time for vitals and meds. Girls were getting their blood pressure checked. Heart rate. Then they had to get on the scale. Several girls sobbed and moaned. Judith had her arm around one of them.

Bluebird, Suzy-Q, and Snapshot came up to me.

"Why are they crying?" I asked.

"Because they're being weighed," Snapshot said as if this was the most obvious thing in the world.

"They're afraid they'll have gained weight," Suzy-Q said. She was holding a pair of pants and a shirt in her arms. She followed my gaze. "Didn't fool them this morning. It depends upon who is doing it. I have to get checked by the doctor. I guess my heart sounds weirder than usual."

"At least you have a heart," Bluebird said.

A girl sobbed loudly. I shivered.

"I wish I could help," I said.

"Why?" Suzy-Q asked.

"Because they're in so much pain."

"It's not your responsibility," Suzy-Q said. "If they can't handle it, it's their problem."

Mia ran up to us—sauntered, really. She wobbled more than ran. "Ready for our walk?" She giggled.

"What are you so excited about?" Bluebird asked. "You haven't eaten anything, so you can't throw anything up."

"Med-eeee-cation, sister."

"Oh yeah," Bluebird said.

"Go get your vits and meds," Suzy-Q said to me. "We'll meet you outside."

Judith took my blood pressure, weighed me. I didn't pay any attention. They had done all this stuff yesterday— only it was a doctor then. Drew blood, too. Urine.

"We're not putting you on any medications yet," Judith said. "We'll wait and see what the blood work says, how your liver is functioning, et cetera. Okay?"

I nodded.

"See you at breakfast."

I went into the dining room, then out the side door, where the girls stood waiting for me, like wasted figures from a surreal painting. Or like Gumby figurines. No, they still looked like creatures from the Day of the Dead.

We started down a trail that led into the desert. After we were about one hundred yards from the center, Mia said, "Sarge—Shelley—is afraid of rattlesnakes, so she won't come very far on this trail. We can purge to our heart's content!"

"It's better to wait until the afternoon," Bluebird said. "When it actually does some good."

"I don't want this fucking medication in my system! It makes me want to eat. It makes me hungry!" Mia snarled like a dog. Or a raccoon. I had startled a raccoon in our garbage one night, and it had sounded— and looked—just like Mia did right this moment.

"Hey," Suzy-Q said. "Quit freaking out. No one here gives a fuck whether you purge until your guts come out. Go for it, girl."

"That's a disgusting visual," Snapshot said.

"It really is," Bluebird said.

All the time, we walked. Into the desert. No other houses. No sound, except maybe an airplane in the distance.

"If I'm not back in twenty, come make sure I haven't passed out." Mia leaped off the path, no longer a raccoon but more like a bighorn sheep I had seen on the Discovery Channel, jumping from rock to rock. Then she was gone.

"I gotta rest," Suzy-Q said, slowly crouching down to the ground until her butt touched the earth. She folded her long, thin legs close to her body. We all sat next to her on the path.

Bluebird chewed her fingernail. "Jesus, Mary, and Rodriguez, I better not get bitten by a scorpion. Or a rattlesnake."

"How long you all been here?" I asked.

"A month," Suzy-Q said. "More or less."

"Fifty-four days," Snapshot said, "but this is my third stint."

"Three weeks," Bluebird said, "and I'm almost ready to go home. I can't wait."

"We can't wait either," Snapshot said. Bluebird stuck her tongue out at her.

"You get used to the routine after a while," Suzy-Q said. "They don't mean any harm. They just don't understand."

"What? What don't they understand?"

"That we're beautiful," Snapshot said.

"They're jealous, really," Suzy-Q said, "because we have been able to attain the ideal. They can't do it. They don't have the self-control. It's like that *Twilight Zone* episode where they're giving this so-called ugly girl plastic surgery so that she'll look like everyone else. Only it turns out that everyone else is really ugly, and she's beautiful. We are that girl."

"Only skinnier," Snapshot said. "She had some meat on her bones."

"But whose idea of beauty is it?" I asked.

"Ours. We've decided that thin is in. Thinners are the winners. Being thin ain't no sin." Snapshot grinned. "Et cetera."

"But the research on anorexia and bulimia indicates it might be caused by a chemical imbalance," I said. "That would mean it wasn't really your choice—this behavior—it was just a chemical reaction to the environment in your body."

"Then it's a good imbalance," Suzy-Q said. "I want to look like this."

"I want to be a ballerina," Bluebird said. "They're so thin. And beautiful."

"Have you ever really looked at ballerinas?" I said. "They don't look like women, really. Women have curves. We have bulges. When we're so skinny, we look androgynous. Or like children. It's almost like the culture wants us to look like men. To be men."

"Well, I ain't no man," Suzy-Q said. "I've got the cunt to prove it."

Bluebird and Snapshot giggled.

"Where is Mia?" Suzy-Q said. "We've got to get in for breakfast."

No one got up to look for Mia. After a few minutes, Suzy-Q pushed herself up, and we started back to the center.

"What about Mia?" I asked.

"Missing-in-action Mia? She'll show up."

"After she throws up," Snapshot said, giggling.

"Aren't you glad you fell in with such a witty crowd?" Suzy-Q said.

"Hey, wait up!" Mia called from behind us. "Jesus, I could have been dead!"

"Better dead then fed," they all recited.

It's personal time. Breakfast was awful. Almost funny in its absurdity. I feel as though I am the adult and all these girls are children. What does that mean? Am I sicker than they are or are they sicker than I am? I'm starting to think like them. Sickness. I am not sick. I am transforming. Like a butterfly. Or a dragonfly.

Something that flies. Because I'm getting these wings.

Girls pushed around food on their plates. Or waited until they thought no one was watching to put it in a napkin or throw it on the floor. Yuck.

Then we all talked about goal setting. The a-dults urged us to mentor one another, to encourage one another to eat. Some of the girls nodded to each other, so maybe some of them are trying to get better. Maybe I should try to get to know them. No one else has come up to introduce herself to me. Although Judith introduced me to the entire group, and then they all said who they were too.

Participants in the Day of the Dead tableau. I couldn't get that image out of my mind.

They talked about relapses.

"Relapses are part of recovery," Judith said. "You'll learn what the warning signs are of a relapse, and then you'll learn how to avoid the relapse."

In a circle we talked about eating, what it meant to us, about our relapses.

I say "we" and "our," but I didn't say a thing. What could I say? "I'm not really one of you, and I think you sound really crazy, and that should worry you because I think I'm an angel."

Next they talked about nutrition. Suzy-Q kept whispering ana jokes in my ear, so I didn't really hear any of it.

I ate some of my breakfast and all of the snack. I put a packet of crackers in my pocket. I felt like my wings needed the nourishment. I know. Sounds strange. But there it is.

In my private counseling session, Judith and the nutritionist—whom they all call Mom—helped me make a menu for my upcoming meals. It made me tired just to think about it.

"I trust you," I finally said. "I'll eat what you give me."

That didn't work. They made me pick what I would eat.

Still later Judith showed me photographs of very skinny women.

"What do you think?" she asked.

"They are very skinny women."

"Do you think they are healthy?"

"No."

She showed me a photograph they had taken of me the day before.

"What do you see?" she asked.

What I didn't see were my wings.

"That's me."

"Do you think you're thin?"

"I am thin," I said, "but nothing like the rest of these girls."

"Why do you suppose some of these girls put such a value in being thin?" she asked.

"I think some people believe it's beautiful," I said. "And it's a control thing. Everything seems out of control, but you can control what goes into your mouth."

Judith nodded.

"Or it's a chemical or hormonal imbalance caused by all the environmental pollution, and it has nothing to do with anything else."

"Which is it?" Judith asked.

"I don't know."

"Some of these girls and women are the best and the brightest in their schools and universities. Why would they want to starve themselves?"

"So they don't have to think about their future or how screwed up the world is and how they have no options and how they're so lucky to be born in this country because if they had been born black in South Africa they would most likely have AIDS. Yet even here, we have to watch out for murder, rape, diseases caused by the degradation of the environment. Although, personally, I think it's a chemical thing."

"Do you want medication?" Judith asked.

"Medication? For what?"

"For your eating disorder."

"I do not have an eating disorder."

It seems as though we talk about food all the time. Or our body image. Self-esteem. I'm not relating to any of it. "I don't belong here!" *I want to scream. Maybe this all would have helped me when I actually had an eating disorder.*

I've waited for guidance. But nada happens.

No divine messages. No wings or dogs or Peter.

Just me in this place.

At lunch they dispensed meds again like they were handing out breath mints. Some of the girls chewed them, to get the sensation of eating without eating.

"When I get home," Bluebird said, "I am going to restrict again. Big-time. And I'll be able to exercise anytime I want.

77

Maybe I'll fast for the month of November. Anyone with me?"

"When are you going home?" I asked.

"Next week, I think," she said. "I kind of wish I was staying through Halloween. I wanted to dress up as a cadaver."

"You wouldn't have to use much makeup," Snapshot said.

After dinner I got to call Mom and Dad. Mom's voice sounded strained, almost shrill. I did not cry or weep or rail. I just told them about the day. I felt distant. Like they were on another planet. I was visiting planet Earth to see if it had any intelligent life. They promised to come visit on Saturday, then Dad had to go back to school. Mom was going to try and find a house to rent in Santa Fe or Taos. Or somewhere in between where I was.

Where was I?

I went to my first twelve-step meeting. The secular version. I didn't know what the nonsecular version was, so it made no difference to me. Behavioral psychologist B. F. Skinner came up with the no-God twelve-steps for alcohol, and then someone changed them to fit eating disorders.

I read the steps off the papers left at the tables in the cafeteria while one of the girls talked.

"Hello, my name is Amy, and I have an eating disorder."

She was translucent, almost. Her skin. Ethereal. Only sickly.

"Hello, Amy," we all said.

I picked up the list of the Twelve Humanist Steps for Eating Disorders:

. . . .

1. We accept the fact that all our efforts to stop our eating disorders have failed.

2. We believe that we must turn elsewhere for help.

3. We turn to our fellow men and women, particularly those who have struggled with the same problem.

4. We have made a list of the situations in which our eating disorder will be triggered.

5. We ask our friends to help us avoid these situations.

6. We are ready to accept the help they give us.

7. We honestly hope they will help.

8. We have made a list of the persons we have harmed and to whom we hope to make amends.

9. We shall do all we can to make amends, in any way that will not cause further harm.

10. We will continue to make such lists and revise them as needed.

11. We appreciate what our friends have done and are doing to help us.

12. We, in turn, are ready to help others who may come to us in the same way.

"These are the Ana twelve steps," Suzy-Q whispered, handing me a humanist twelve steps piece of paper she had marked up.

"Before I came here, I had no control over my eating disorder," Amy said. "But I wouldn't admit it to anyone. I thought I was better than everyone in my family because I could control my eating, and they all seemed like such pigs."

"Ana's 8 Steps (We Do It Quicker)," Suzy-Q had written. Then she had crossed out certain words and added others so the steps read:

. . . .

1. We accept the fact that all your efforts to stop our eating disorders have failed.

2. We believe that you must turn elsewhere for help.

3. We turn to our fellow anas and mias, particularly those who have struggled with the same problem.

4. We have made a list of the situations in which we will most likely eat.

5. We ask our friends to help us avoid these situations.

6. We are ready to accept the help they give us in this matter.

7. We honestly hope they can help us.

8. We, in turn, are ready to help others who may come to us in the same way.

"Thank you," Amy said. The audience of skin and bones clapped for her. A strange sound. More like drumming than clapping. Made me shiver.

I couldn't sleep. I listened for Suzy-Q's sleep breathing but couldn't hear it. I tried to see in the darkness. Was she in her bed? It didn't matter. I got up and quietly opened the door and slipped out into the hallway. The lights were dim but still too bright on the shiny floor. I stood for a second, listening. Nothing. My bare feet slapped noisily against the linoleum as I wandered by the living room, then the cafeteria. I glanced into each room. No one. Could it be I was the only one awake? My back itched, and I reached over my shoulder. I still couldn't feel the nubs. And I was hungry. No, no, I couldn't be hungry. I had eaten. A little today.

I was standing at the door to the kitchen. Judith had told me it was locked, to prevent bingeing. But it was open a crack.

The crack of doom.

I slipped into the darkness and closed the door behind me. I heard something rustle. Mice? I waited for my eyes to adjust. Then I went around the island toward the tall white cupboards. On the floor someone huddled.

"Get down," the huddle whispered. "They shine lights in here."

I crouched next to the girl. She looked up at me, holding on to a bag of something.

"Mia," I said. "You left the door open."

"Oops." She reached her hand into the bag and pulled out several crackers and stuffed them in her mouth. "You want some?" she asked, her mouth so full I could barely understand her.

I nodded, sat on the floor, and leaned my back against the cupboards. Mia pulled out another handful of crackers and gave them to me. I took one and lightly bit the edges of it.

Mia chewed, her cheeks bulging out, making her look like a chipmunk. I wanted to laugh, except it wasn't funny.

Mia wiped the back of her hand across her mouth. "Man, I needed that."

"I didn't know you ate," I whispered.

"Yeah, well, sometimes I does, sometimes I don'ts." She giggled. "Better than drink, better than sex. High on large quantities of carbs. I've got night eating syndrome, they say. That's one of my many, many syndromes. Along with anorexia. Or bulimia. It depends on the day of the week."

I had seen info on that when I looked at the sites on eating disorders.

"Apparently depression, anxiety, boredom, and stress can trigger it." Mia laughed quietly. "Which do you think it is, Tammy dear? Is it the anxiety from being in this hellhole? Actually, it gives hell a bad name 'cause it looks so nice, doesn't it? And they're all so nice. A bunch of fucking Stepford anorexics, if you ask me. Could it be the depression? My boyfriend, Michael, have I told you about him? He's getting tired of waiting for me and says he's gonna screw someone else if I don't get out of here. So he's been coming here, and he fucks me out there, by the cactus, scorpions, and coyotes. It's not as bad as when my uncle used to fuck me, but almost. And stress? I feel no stress. I feel nothing. I am perfectly content. So content. Aren't you, Tammy?"

"Well, I—"

"I don't feel so good," Mia said. "Of course, there's no place to throw up. Unless I want to go outside. But I don't feel like communing with the rattlesnakes. Ugh." Mia started to get up, then sat back down.

"Night eating syndrome is a disease and cannot be cured with willpower alone," Mia said. "That's what they say about them all, isn't it? Anorexia is a disease and cannot be cured with willpower alone. Mia is a disease, and she cannot be cured with willpower alone. What about willpower together? Then could it be cured?" She pushed herself up, wobbled a bit, then stumbled toward the door, dropping the bag of crackers as she went. "Mia is a disease, and she cannot be cured with willpower alone. Mia is a disease, and she cannot . . ."

I thought about going after her, but I was suddenly so exhausted I could hardly move. I reached for the crackers and ate a few, hoping my wings were getting the nourishment they needed. Then I got up and went back to my room.

I looked over at Suzy-Q's bed. It was empty. I listened. Then I went over to the closed closet door. This time it sounded like she was crying.

"Are you okay in there?" I asked Suzy-Q.

The door opened. Darkness.

"Just exercising. But it hurts. You want to join me?"

"Maybe another time."

"Okay." The door shut.

I dreamed of the whisper of wings.

Suzy-Q was right. You get used to the routine. It's almost comforting. Better for me because I'm not always looking for ways to throw up, like the others. Although I don't eat all of my food, I eat some of it. That seems to please the a-dults. And I've gained some weight. This fact does not cause me to scream or sob. At night I have to sleep on my side or belly because the wings are uncomfortable.

"Still can't see them, darlin'," Suzy-Q tells me.

I like the art therapy classes. They have equine therapy. I might try that. Hang out with the horses. We don't actually ride them. I guess we just take care of them. Suzy-Q said there was no way she was shoveling anyone's shit, especially an animal that could shit that big.

I've never had friends like these, but they are the best part of Mercywood. Mia is happy one moment, crazy angry the next. Bluebird acts laid back, but she's snappy; passive-aggressive, I think they call it. She's scared about going home. Snapshot has the best wit of just about anyone I've ever met, except maybe Suzy-Q and my mom. They're smart, too, although sometimes their knowledge of anorexia and bulimia is nauseating.

One morning after lunch Suzy-Q whispered, "They do experimental stuff here too."

"Yeah, like Frankenstein stuff," Snapshot said. "If you don't watch out, they'll do it to you, too."

Mia rolled her eyes. "They're just trying to scare you."

"Are they force-feeding people?" I asked.

"Worse," Suzy-Q said. "Come on."

We walked to a part of the treatment center I had not been in. No one tried to stop us, so I wasn't afraid, even though Suzy-Q kept making strange "woo-woo" noises. Eventually we stopped at a green door. Suzy-Q opened it, and we went inside. It felt like a sauna it was so hot. Bluebird was sitting in a recliner, along with several other girls. Soothing music played in the background.

"This doesn't look so bad," I said.

Bluebird half smiled when she saw us. We went and stood around her.

"How's it goin', toots?" Suzy-Q asked.

"It's very nice," Bluebird said.

"See, I told you it was frightening."

"What is this?" I asked. "Why is it so hot in here?"

"Some researcher discovered that anorexics have a low body temperature. So they're trying to treat my symptoms. After I eat, I come in here sometimes. To get warm. And I have to keep still. No exercise."

"Maybe it's like going back to the womb," Snapshot said.

"Does it make you want to eat?" Mia asked.

Bluebird shook her head. "It's just kind of . . . quieting. You know? I don't feel so . . ." She stopped.

"Compulsive?" Mia asked.

Bluebird nodded. "Yeah, that's it. Like the chattering in my head is quieting down."

"That's 'cause it's so freaking hot in here," Suzy-Q said. "Who could think in this heat?"

"Maybe that's the key to it all, then," Snapshot said. "We've all gotta stop thinking."

Every day is filled with weeks and weeks of activity and experiences, it seems. Everyone is in so much pain. Except me. I am the most pain-free. Painless. How would I describe it? Lily White, can you help me? No. I can't get online. No help at all. I don't think I'm as wrecked as they all are. They may not even put me on any meds.

"So go ahead and ask us how we came to be like this," Mia said one morning as we sat on the desert path before breakfast.

"OK. How did you get to be like this?" I asked.

"Well, maybe not how, but when. Who knows how? We're just gifted." Mia grinned.

"My parents divorced and the kids in school started calling me fat," Bluebird said. "That's when I started. The eating was soooo nice, but then I had the same problem I had before I started, only now I was fat. So I started puking it up."

"Yeah, a couple of boys in school started calling me fat," Mia said. "This was right after my uncle molested me. Why do they call it that? Molest. It seems like such a nice word. Really. He fucking raped me. Now I fuck one of those boys who used to call me fat. I think he really likes boys because he wants me skinnier and skinnier. 'I can still see your tits,' he says as he's fucking me."

Snapshot shrugged. "Who knows? I was about nine and felt depressed about something. I just stopped feeling hungry. Then everyone made such a fuss, and it was a challenge to me to keep from doing what they wanted me to do. I guess. After that initial phase of not eating, I just never felt exactly right again. Something."

"I never had a good relationship with food," Suzy-Q said. "My body never liked it. What about you, Tammy true?"

"A little over a year ago a bunch of things happened, and I just kept eating and eating. I was about to go into high school, and I was suddenly afraid I was fat and I wouldn't fit in. I started really monitoring what I ate. But sometimes I just got so hungry. So then I'd throw up."

"When did you decide you were becoming an angel?" Suzy-Q asked.

"I'm not really sure," I said. "I was watching the news, and it suddenly occurred to me—listening to all these talking heads—that people didn't seem to have any compassion and didn't show one another any mercy. Especially these people who claimed to be religious. I thought their god must be a real creep to have follow-ers like them. They didn't listen. They lied about things. I thought about all the wars, AIDS, pollution. My mom was in the next room using her inhaler because she was having trouble breathing. On the news they were mentioning the AIDS orphans. Just mentioning it. Just a line or two. Something like 14 million AIDS orphans. And most of these children are in Africa and don't have other relatives who can help them. They lose their parents, and then they starve to death or go into prostitution or anything to survive. I thought, 'What kind of world allows these things to happen? What kind of people allow the destruction of their homeland—the Earth—because of greed?' I started to cry. I went to bed crying. I dreamed I was leaning over someone, someone dying, my wings stretched out like an umbrella over the two of us, and I was whispering—bestowing compassion and mercy in a world that really needs it."

"The dream told you you were an angel?" Bluebird asked.

"Yeah, and the fact that my back itched, and I could feel the wings growing."

"So because you were getting wings, you think you're an angel?" Suzy-Q said. "Why not a bird or a fairy, even a freaking mosquito? An angel sounds so religious. Is this some kind of religious conversion?"

Hmmm. I had not thought of that.

"Do you believe in God?" Bluebird asked. "We're supposed to turn ourselves over to God in the real Twelve Steps."

"I'm not turning myself over to some fascist with a white beard telling me what I can and cannot be," Mia Said. "He was just invented by men anyway."

"I don't believe in God the way people talk about God," I

said. "And they usually say 'him' and then claim that they don't really see God as a he or a she, and I say, 'Then, why do you use he?'"

"But what does eating or not eating have to do with being an angel?" Suzy-Q asked.

"Angels don't have to eat, do they? I mean, they're not human," I said.

"Horses aren't human," Suzy-Q said, "but they eat."

"That's true," I said. "When my grandmother was about my age, she almost starved to death, but it wasn't her choice. She was in a concentration camp."

"Wow," Bluebird said. "That's horrible."

"She doesn't talk about it much, but she says that when people are starving, or fighting for their lives, they do terrible things. Mom said she went on a diet once when she was a teenager, and Grandma slapped her across the face, reminding her of how many people from her family had actually starved to death."

"Maybe you're just acting out something from your grandma's life," Bluebird said. "Maybe we all are somehow."

"What do you mean?" I asked.

"You could be a chimera," she said. "Many of us have more than one DNA in us. They've found this out recently. I mean the DNA of more than one person. This woman was having kidney problems and needed a transplant. Her three sons went in to get tested. The test results came back saying the father was the father but this woman was not the mother, which was impossible, since she had given birth to the children. Well, it turned out that her blood had one type of DNA, and her ovaries—where her sons' DNA had come from—had another type of DNA. So what they think now is that the DNA from our mothers, maybe our grandmothers, can migrate to us while we're in the womb, and our DNA can migrate to our mother. Maybe having several peoples' wandering DNA may cause us to do all sorts of things and act in all sorts of ways that we don't understand."

"That's creepy, thinking I may have my mother's DNA floating around in me," Mia said, "telling me what to do."

"Maybe Tammy is reliving her grandmother almost starving to death," Bluebird said, "and the DNA is making her act it out like a movie."

"What about the rest of us?" Snapshot asked.

"The rest of us are just fucking crazy," Suzy-Q said.

"If I was starving, like your grandmother was," Mia said. "I would do anything. I would kill people. I would lie, steal. I would do anything to save my life and get that food so I wouldn't starve to death."

I pulled a package of crackers from my pocket and held them out to her.

"You don't have to kill, steal, or lie," I said. "You are welcome to it."

Mia stared at my hand, at the crackers, for several moments.

"Metaphorically speaking, of course," she said. "I am not starving to death. I am starving to beauty. So there!"

"Did you ever see the movie King of Hearts?" I asked.

They shook their heads.

"It's a great antiwar movie. A soldier goes to a French village and finds these people from the lunatic asylum have taken over after the 'normal' villagers left. The soldier spends most of the movie trying to get the crazy people to leave too. They won't go, but they want him to stay and be their king. The 'normal' villagers return, and the crazy people go back to the loony bin. In the end the soldier walks away from his army buds, taking off his rifle and clothes, until he is standing in front of the lunatic asylum, naked. I feel that way. Like so much of the world is insane. You know what I mean?"

They all nodded.

"Do you want to be our Queen of Hearts?" Suzy-Q asked.

"You *are* already the queen!" I said.

She shook her head. "I'm the Queen of the Disordered. Queen of the Skinny Assed. You be our Queen of Hearts."

"Does that mean I have to stay in the loony bin with you all?"

"Absolutely."

We all stood. Suzy-Q put me in the middle of the four of them.

"We, the Fabulous Five," Suzy-Q said, "dub you, Tammy, The Angel Mercy, as the Queen of Hearts. Our Queen of Hearts specifically."

They each put a hand on my shoulder and said all together, "We, the Fabulous Five, dub you, Tammy, The Angel Mercy, as our Queen of Hearts."

"May you have mercy on our souls," Suzy-Q added, "and our bodacious bods."

We all clapped.

"Now strip," Suzy-Q said.

"What?"

"Take your clothes off," she said. "You said the soldier went to the asylum naked. You gotta do it, sister, if you're gonna be our Queen of Hearts."

"Abso-fucking-lutely!" Mia said. The other two girls clapped.

"Not really," I said.

"Really," they said.

So as they hooted and hollered, I took off my clothes, then ran to the door of the center, naked. I turned to look at them. They bowed, and I quickly ran back and got dressed again.

Was it Amy? She collapsed tonight. Fell to the floor like a little rag doll. We stared at her. Then someone ran for the phone. An ambulance came, and they took her away. I started to shake and couldn't stop. I hadn't done anything to help her. I just stared, like all the rest of them. How could I believe there was something special about me? That I had wings? That I was an angel? How ridiculous is that in the face of everything! I have no ability. I am completely helpless to change anything. To help anyone.

Will anyone help me?

The five of us spent as much time as we could outside. We walked the path leading away from the institute and into the desert. We stayed on the path, since most of them were afraid of snakes, scorpions, and other little nasties. I didn't know if I was afraid, but I stayed on the path too, for the most part. When the path dipped with the decline of the hill, and the center was no longer in sight, we all breathed deeply, as if truly breathing for the first time all day. Sarge never followed us. No one ever followed us. We stood on the hills, which were dotted with clumps of evergreens, and stared. The hills were red, like a Georgia O'Keeffe painting, and we were clumps too, or pillars, looking to the east. (Or was it north?) Looking for something.

Early one evening during our break when we were out on the hills, a coyote dashed right in front of us. She stopped, turned to look at us, then sprung away again, reminding me of a deer inside of a canine. Coyotes are shape-shifters, though, so she could have been anything. Suzy-Q stepped off the path and followed her.

And we followed Suzy-Q. The sun was setting, so the hills were beginning to turn golden red. We all had a pink tinge, even the coyote, who disappeared over a ridge. Soon we stood on the edge looking down at a small ruined church atop another hill. The steeple was still whole, three walls stood, and the roof covered it all.

"Look," Snapshot said, pointing. We followed the line of her arm, to the left of the church, to another hillside, where five shirtless men stood facing the sun while they struck themselves on the back with what looked like cat-o'-nine-tails.

"Kinky," Suzy-Q said.

"I'd heard about them," Snapshot said, "the last time I was here, but I didn't believe it was true. They're called *Los Hermanos Penitentes*."

"I guess so," Suzy-Q said.

"What is that?" Bluebird asked.

"They're flagellants," I said. "They beat themselves— and others, I think—because they believe they're sinful."

"Is that why?" Suzy-Q asked.

I shrugged. "I guess."

"It's disgusting," Mia said. "They hate the human body, their own human body, because they were born from a woman, so they're punishing themselves."

"Well, what are we doing?" Bluebird asked. "Don't we hate our bodies? Aren't we punishing our bodies?"

"Not because we were born from a woman!" Mia said.

Suzy-Q laughed. "Poor boys. Looks like they don't eat either. Maybe we should meet and start a cult together. The Beat and Not Eat cult."

"That's sick," Snapshot said.

"It really is," Suzy-Q said. She started down the hill toward the partially ruined church. We followed. Mia craned her neck to keep the penitents in view. As we got close to the church, I could see the roof of the church was ready to collapse, along with at least two of the walls.

"Dust to dust," Suzy-Q said. "It's about time. That institution has made a mess of things." She started to step inside the ruins when a priest or a monk—a man dressed in brown robes—appeared from around the corner, his hands lightly folded in front of his chest.

"Sisters," he said. "Welcome. You are penitents too?"

"What'd he say?" Bluebird asked.

The others shrugged.

"He welcomed us," I said. "Couldn't you understand him?"

"He's not speaking English, honey," Suzy-Q said. "That's the only language we know, besides the language of hunger."

I frowned. But I had understood him. I knew some Spanish and German. Had he spoken Spanish?

"He also asked if we were penitents."

"Ha!" Mia said.

"Why do you ask, Father?" I said.

"Because you are not of the body," he said.

I looked at my friends. They stared blankly.

"What do you mean?" I asked.

"Not of the flesh," he said. He smiled benignly, but he didn't seem to be all there.

I frowned. "You mean because we don't eat?"

He nodded.

I relayed this bit of conversation to the girls.

"We are definitely of the body," Mia said, "you perverted psycho."

The monk smiled.

"He doesn't understand us, either," Bluebird said.

"Hmmm," Suzy-Q said. "Thanks, Pops. We'll just look around." She leaned into the church. "Looks a bit fragile."

"Hey, look at that rock up there," Bluebird said. "I bet we'd get quite a view from up there. Better than an old church."

Suzy-Q and Snapshot followed Bluebird up the hill. I glanced around for Mia but didn't see her. The monk still smiled at me.

"Do you see the wings?" I asked.

He cocked his head. "Wings?"

"Never mind."

I scrambled up the hill after the girls. Soon the four of us were standing on a large, flat rock looking out at the hills and the valley below, which was almost black now that the sun was nearly down.

Snapshot started to sing and dance.

"Women in ancient Greece used to go out onto mountaintops and celebrate together," I said. "I wonder if it was like this. One group was called the maenads, or 'the mad women.'"

"Yes! The mad women!" Snapshot cried.

"The story goes they made mead, drank it, and danced under the moon in honor of Dionysus or Pan, but I think they really worshipped the goddess. And ecstasy."

"They had Ecstasy back then?" Bluebird asked.

"Not the drug, you dim bulb," Suzy-Q said. "The actual feeling of *ecstasy*."

"I may be a dim bulb, but you're a half watt," Bluebird said, dancing on the stone next to Snapshot.

Suzy-Q groaned.

"My mom used to tell me the story of the women of Amphissa," I said. "The maenads were up on the mountain dancing and having a good ole time, and it got late. They stumbled off the mountain—drunk on their ecstatic dances and rituals—and into the town of Amphissa, which was occupied at that time by a group of soldiers. Well, the older women in town saw these maenads and were afraid the soldiers might hurt the altered women. So the women surrounded the maenads as they slept, they circled them, and kept watch over them until morning. When the young women awakened, the women protecting them gave them food and water."

Bluebird and Snapshot had stopped dancing to listen.

"What a great story," they said in unison.

Suzy-Q put her hands on her hips. "Well, I think one of our mad women might need protecting right now."

We followed her gaze. Mia danced in front of the flagellant men, who were no longer flagellating because they were staring at the naked, dancing woman in front of them.

We hopped off our rock and hurried down the hill and up again, until we were beside the dancing Mia. Suzy-Q grabbed her while we picked up her clothes, and then we dragged her away.

"The human body is a beautiful thing! Don't fuck with it!" Mia screamed.

"Nice to meet you, boys," Suzy-Q called over her shoulder.

Laughing, we ran away. I glanced back. The men were once again whipping themselves.

"Jack-offs," Mia said as she stopped to put on her clothes.

"If only they did," Bluebird said.

"That's probably why they're whipping themselves," Suzy-Q said.

"That and the fact they're crazy motherfuckers," Bluebird said.

One night the five of us sat outside in the cool October air counting stars, until Mia's disgusting boyfriend showed up and she sneaked away to have sex with him. I didn't understand it, but I didn't have to. It was her business.

"What are those beads around your wrist?" Mia asked.

I unwrapped the mala and held it up.

"My aunt Lenny gave it to me," I said. "You touch a bead and recite a mantra. It's kind of like a prayer or a meditation. Aunt Lenny calls upon Nature and the goddess to help her get through the day."

"Isn't that Buddhist?" Bluebird asked, looking at the mala.

I nodded. "Buddhists use them, but this method of reciting is very old. Muslims use a similar device. Catholics use rosaries. I like it because it reminds me of my aunt."

"What do you recite?" Mia asked.

"Om Tara tu tare ture soha. It's a chant to the goddess Tara, She Who Hears the Cries of the World."

"She hears the cries of the world?" Suzy-Q asked. "And then what? Does she try to help? Or does she just listen."

The other girls laughed.

"My aunt says that Tara has stayed on Earth and tries to alleviate suffering," I said.

"Looks like it's working," Suzy-Q said.

"Is that called irony?" Bluebird asked. She grinned.

"At least Tara's trying," I said. "I guess. It does seem kind of hopeless."

"You think we should all be nice to each other, don't you?" Suzy-Q said.

"No, not nice," I said. "But kindness. Compassion. Being

nice seems fakey to me. Like getting along just to get along. The word kindness *comes from the word kin. So being kind is treating others like they are your kin. People seem so nasty just to be nasty. They're always so sure they're right. Even my parents: They're so sure I have an eating disorder that they won't even consider something else is going on."

"You think you have to save the world, don't you?" Suzy-Q asked.

"No, my mom thinks she has to save the world. I know I can't."

"But an angel could," Suzy-Q said.

"Well, I figure an angel would be given particular tasks, right? So I would know what to do to help, to fix, to save, whatever."

"But you said you don't believe in God," Bluebird said. "Who's going to give you these tasks?"

"I don't know," I said. "As soon as my wings are grown and they unfurl, I'll know everything."

Suzy-Q laughed. "Wouldn't life be grand if it were that simple?"

"Look," Snapshot said. "A falling star. Just like all of us. Burning out."

"After hanging around in space for a few million years, give or take," I said.

"Wow," she said. "Do you think if we breathe in the dust from the falling star, we could live a million years too?"

"Maybe," I said.

"Why would you want to live for a million years?" Bluebird asked.

In art therapy class we were asked to "express our eating disorder creatively." Most of the girls stood at their easels splashing paint onto paper. Some got globs of clay and began kneading them like bread dough. Suzy-Q drew black dots on a huge piece of paper. Snapshot drew squares—like photographs—then sketched in people making faces. Bluebird stood at the table staring up at the ceiling.

"What are you doing?" the teacher asked.

"I'm thinking, I'm thinking," Bluebird said.

"Try to feel it," the teacher said. "Don't intellectual-ize it."

I saw Bluebird grit her teeth. She wanted to say something nasty to the teacher, but she didn't. She was so nervous about going home, and everything seemed to irritate her.

"Mercy, what about you?" the teacher asked.

I shrugged.

"She's feeling it, Teach," Suzy-Q said. "She's feeling it!"

The room was humming like a veritable hive of busy bees. Movement, energy. Maybe even a hint of rebellion. Except for Bluebird. She was completely still.

Then she walked to the middle of the room, looked at

the ceiling again, and opened her mouth. . . .

And let out a piercing scream. I covered my ears and cringed. Everyone did. And then the pitch leveled off, so that it was one long, gorgeous, pitiful note. It was the saddest thing I had ever heard.

The teacher called out Bluebird's name, even stepped toward her. The four of us jumped up and surrounded Bluebird, holding hands, until she was finished. Then we all stood silently as the teacher and the other girls looked at us.

Finally the teacher said, "That was very creative. Thank you."

I think she even wiped away a tear. I know I did. The scream reverberated in my chest for a long while, like a low hum you hear all day but whose source you can't really identify. Even after I lay in bed trying to sleep, I felt it. I opened my mouth, thinking that would relieve it, but nothing came out. Not a sigh, whimper, cry. Nothing.

In the morning it was gone.

After health check one morning they took Suzy-Q away. We tried to visit her in the infirmary, but they wouldn't let us. I wondered if they were force-feeding her.

"I hear they stick a tube down your throat," Snapshot said.

"No, they don't do that anymore," Mia said.

"She's probably just on an IV," Bluebird said.

"They should let us see her at least," Snapshot said.

"Why? We've done her a helluva lot of good so far."

Finally, after several days, Suzy-Q came back to us.

"If that place is called the infirmary, is this the firmary?" she asked.

"Same ole Suzy-Q," Bluebird said. "Thank goodness."

"What was wrong?" I asked.

She lay on her bed, her head against the pillow. She looked like a tired old little girl.

"I can't imagine," Suzy-Q said. "Maybe something to do with me starving myself to death."

One night Mia's boyfriend gave her a bottle of gin, and she sneaked it into the center. We saved it for the Friday night before Bluebird was leaving. Then my four friends drank it until they were drunk—which didn't take much. I took a couple of swigs, but I didn't like the smell. I felt a bit tipsy—I guess. I had never had liquor before. The five of us sat in our room giggling until long after lights-out.

"When I grow up," Bluebird said, swinging the bottle around above her head as we all sat on the floor, trying to be quiet, "I want to be as thin as Suzy-Q."

"No, no," Mia said, grabbing the empty bottle from Bluebird, "when I grow up, I want to be Suzy-Q."

"Who wants to grow up?" Snapshot said. "Throw up, yes, grow up, nada."

Suzy-Q leaned against her bed and grinned.

"If you could change anything in your life right this minute, what would you change?" Bluebird asked. She was slurring her words. Moonlight streamed through the window, filling the dark room with a kind of milky starlight—with stars floating around us like dust motes. I kept reaching up to catch one.

"I would change the color of my eyes," Mia said. "So that they looked like Tammy's. She has sky-colored eyes. New Mexico sky colored."

"Yeah, Tammy's eyes. They are filled with Mercy," Snapshot said. We laughed quietly.

"We're all going to get in big trouble," Mia said, "if we're caught."

"Except me," Bluebird said, "since I'm already going home."

"That's right," Mia said. "What are they going to do? Kick us out? Send us to bed without our supper? Well then, let's make some more noise!"

"What would you change, Suzy-Q?" Bluebird asked.

"Everything," she said.

"Shit," Snapshot said. "I hear footsteps."

We all held our breath.

The footsteps got louder. Then quieter.

We breathed again, accidentally breathing in starlight.

"We better go to bed," Mia said.

The three drunken girls got up noisily, left our room, and wobbled away.

Suzy-Q and I crawled into our beds.

"Crazy kids," Suzy-Q said.

"Yeah."

She sighed.

"You OK?" I asked.

"They want to be like me," Suzy-Q said, "which is ridiculous. They don't know anything about me."

"What do you mean?"

"I'm not a model," she said. "Not really. I was a schoolteacher, but they fired me because they said I was too skinny. They didn't say that, but they did say my 'eating disorder' was negatively impacting the children. After that I looked for modeling work. I got a few gigs. Not a lot. The heroin-chic look is over, I guess. I can't get hired teaching again. Everyone thinks I'm a bad influence, especially on girls. Can you imagine? Just by looking at me they can become damaged!" She cried softly.

"I don't want to be this way, Mercy," she whispered. "I want to eat. I really want to. But I can't make myself. This terrible panic sets in—like if I eat, I will die. I don't think I'm beautiful. I think I look like someone who was in a concentration camp. I don't think it's normal. That chemical thing you were talking about. I think maybe that's it. But the medication hasn't worked for me. I still can't eat. Did you ever read Kafka's A Hunger Artist? *This guy starves himself for the entertainment of others, but no one really pays any attention to him, and finally, after he gets their admiration, he admits that he fasted because he couldn't find the food he wanted. 'Believe me,' he says, 'if I had found the food I liked, I would have feasted.' That's the way I feel, Mercy. I want to feast!"*

"So why do you tell the other girls that they're normal? That it's OK to starve themselves?"

"Maybe it is OK for them. Maybe. I don't know. I just know I wish I could change everything."

I was quiet for a few moments, waiting for her to go on, until I realized she was breathing deeply—sleep breathing.

Then I heard her from out of the darkness, "Still can't see them, The Angel Mercy."

The four of us said good-bye to Bluebird before breakfast the next morning. The girls looked paler than normal. Bluebird cried. Suzy-Q told her to get her ass moving. After she left, after the car had driven her away, Suzy-Q looked at each of us, then said, "We look like extras from a Vampire Lestat book."

Later in the day my parents came and we had family therapy. I don't remember much about it, except the docs decided I didn't need meds right now, besides some nutritional supplements. My parents seemed pleased with that. I was tired. And distant. I watched my parents and the therapist and tried to listen while they talked, but nothing seemed to register. I wanted to get back to my friends. I missed Bluebird already. Suzy-Q was looking for someone else we could take under our wings.

"Or under your wings," she said. "You are the angel, after all."

Two newbies were coming tomorrow.

I walked Mom and Dad out to the car.

"You can go home too, Mom," I said. "I'm OK here alone."

"You really like your new friends?" Mom asked.

I nodded. I had not given my parentals much detail about any of the girls since that first day, when I said none of them wanted to get better. I knew even my liberal parents would think the Fab Four—Fab Three now—were a little bit whacked.

"They say you are doing remarkably well," Dad said. "Except that you won't admit you have an eating disorder."

"I know," I said. "I'm working on that."

Upon advice from Suzy-Q. She told me just to act whatever way they wanted me to act. If I could act "normal," they would pay less attention to me.

"It's like the legal system," she said. "If you're really not guilty of a crime and you keep saying you are innocent, you'll get more time than someone who cops to it, guilty or not. They want repentance. They want to know that you understand you are not acting within their parameters of what is normal."

I was trying. I spoke up at a few group discussions. Tried to talk about my relationship with food a couple of times. I had not been able to stand up and say, "Hi, I'm Mercy, and I have an eating disorder."

"Hello, Mercy."

"If you really don't want me to stay," Mom said, "I'll go home. I can be back here in a few hours if you need me."

"Go back and save the world," I said.

"I don't care about the world," she said, hugging me. "I just care about you."

. . . .

"Mercy."

I opened my eyes. Peter sat on the end of my bed.

"What?" I asked.

"Be prepared," he said.

Then he was gone, riding a moonbeam out the window.

"Let's go," Suzy-Q said. "We've got a newbie coming in. Let's see if she is one of us."

"How do we decide that?" I asked.

We were getting dressed. Suzy-Q flinched a couple of times as she pulled a sweatshirt over her head.

"It's a certain look," Suzy-Q said.

I laughed. "You just check them out to see if you're still the skinniest. Still the reigning queen."

"Yeah, you're right."

We started walking down the hall. Snapshot and Mia joined us.

"What's the plan, Stan?" Mia asked.

"Well, I think—" Suzy-Q started. "Oh." She stopped.

"What's wrong?" I asked.

"I think—"

She collapsed, hitting the floor with a *thud*. A peculiar sound. A peculiar sight. Like all the air had suddenly gone out of a balloon. Or the string holding up the skeleton had suddenly been cut.

I knelt on the floor beside her. She was smiling.

Snapshot screamed.

"Help!" Mia called. Then her footsteps. Running, running. "Help!"

"Funny, the world looks different from down here," Suzy-Q said. "I can't breathe," she whispered. She was translucent, transfigured. Transformed.

She reached for my hand.

"Your eyes are so blue," Suzy-Q said to me. "Like the world. I feel as though I'm in a boat rowing. Rowing to you."

"It's okay," I said.

"Don't tell them," she whispered. "Let them believe it was all true."

"Do you think that's best?" I asked.

"No," she whispered. "I feel light as a feather. Finally."

"Hang on," I said.

She smiled. "Mercy."

"What?"

"I can see them. Hear them."

"What?"

"Your wings, darlin'. I see you've finally got your wings."

Suzy-Q breathed out, and I breathed in her exhale. I was certain I tasted stardust. I waited for another breath, for another taste of the universe.

Snapshot began sobbing. "She's dead, she's dead."

part three

"What happened?" Shelley asked as the EMTs put Suzy-Q on the stretcher and carried her out of the building.

Skeletons masquerading as girls clung to one another, crying, licking their faces for the salt, their hands fluttering.

"Wow, I was so wrong." Suzy-Q stood next to Peter. He reached up for her hand. "I'm starving," she said.

"No lie," Peter said.

"Where's Mercy?" Nancy asked as she and George hurried into the center.

"I'm afraid she was with Suzanne Lassiter when it happened," Judith Gardner said.

"So her name was really Suzy?" Mia whispered to Snapshot.

"Is she all right?" George asked.

"Suzanne or Mercy?"

"Where is Mercy!" Nancy was shouting.

"Well, no one has seen her since—," Judith began.

"My daughter is missing?" Nancy said. "Mercy!" she screamed.

"I'm sure she's here somewhere, nearby," Judith said. "She couldn't have gone far."

"I guess she doesn't know about the wings," Snapshot whispered. "Look, it's snowing."

The two girls went outside, tilted their heads back, and opened their mouths.

"Zero calories," Mia said.

Mary washed her hands in the sink and looked out the kitchen of the Big House. Beyond the fence was Hopi land and the Pueblo, although she couldn't see the Pueblo from here. The leaves covered the ground near the house, then the desert took over, dark blond, dotted with brush until it reached the mountains. Mary couldn't remember why the Hopis and the Mabel Dodge Luhan House had argued with each other—why the fence had come to be put up. It had happened before her time—or before she cared about such matters. Sometimes she longed to step over the fence, look toward where she knew Blue Lake was, and spread her arms out wide. Of course, she could just go to the

Pueblo, or Blue Lake, since she was Hopi, but the fence bothered her. She turned off the water and shook her hands over the sink. She squinted. Looked like someone was out on the land. Mary reached for the dish towel and wiped her hands on it. Probably just someone's dog. Too many dogs wandering all over Taos making mischief. Pueblo dogs were mostly all right. But white people's dogs were just crazy.

"Hey, Mary." Carl came into the kitchen from the back door. "How's breakfast?"

She nodded toward the stainless steel countertop where she had left Carl a plate.

"Never a beggar or a borrower be," he said, even though he was both, Mary thought. "Thank you, Mary, Mary." He rubbed his hands together as he went toward the food.

Mary had never seen a person who was hungry as often as Carl was. Like so many single men she knew, he couldn't take care of himself to save his life. She hoped she and her husband had taught their children better.

Carl grabbed the fork next to the plate and began shoveling eggs and potatoes into his mouth.

"Oh, Mary! You have outdone yourself!" He closed his eyes and moaned.

And talk. He could talk a dead horse dead again.

He came over to stand next to her while he looked

out the window. She stepped a bit away from him. Carl did not really understand personal space. But he was an interesting fellow, and she kind of liked him.

"I wish they'd let me use the blower," he said. "I could get those leaves taken care of a lot faster. Granted, it's noisy and it pollutes. Beautiful day, though. Maybe I'll take off and do some fishing. Hey."

Mary turned around and looked out the window again, following Carl's gaze.

Someone *was* on the Hopi land.

"It's a girl," Carl said.

The girl was facing the sacred mountains.

"She's naked," Carl said. "And she has wings!"

Mary leaned toward the window and blinked. Must be a trick of light.

She hurried to the freezer room, grabbed her jacket, and went out the back door, followed by Carl. She opened the gate that led around to the back of the house, then stood at the other gate, waiting for Carl to find the right key to the lock.

"Goddamn stupid thing," he mumbled as he went around his huge key ring. He tried several keys. None worked.

Mary heard the fluttering of wings. Carl stopped and looked around. "Maybe we should call someone," he said.

"That one," Mary said, pointing to a key on the ring.

Carl tried it, the padlock opened.

"Why didn't you just say so?" Carl said.

"I did."

Carl opened the gate, and the two of them went onto Hopi land. The girl still faced the mountains. No wings, though. Must have been the light. She held something in her left hand.

"Hello," Mary said softly as they neared the girl.

The girl turned around slowly. She held a small laptop computer in her left hand.

The girl smiled. "An apple a day keeps the doctor away."

"Do you want an apple?" Mary asked.

"Only if I can eat it," the girl said.

She looked to be about thirteen years old. Or much older. She was thin. Her eyes were the color of the sky. Or the oceans viewed from above the Earth. Mary wasn't sure which. Her eyes seemed to be changing color. Carl's mouth was wide open.

"Carl," Mary said.

Carl looked down at the ground. "I'm so sorry," he said.

Mary went closer to the girl and saw that she was trembling, like a rabbit about to bolt.

"You must be cold," Mary said. "Would you like my

jacket?" She carefully laid her coat across the girl's shoulders.

"I am Mary, this is Carl," Mary said. "What's your name?"

The girl blinked. "I've forgotten."

part four

I'm sitting on the couch in the Big Room of the Big House, my bandaged feet tucked under the blanket Carl spread over me. Natasha is in the office nearby. She's the manager, Carl told me, and is the one who gave permission for them to bring me back here after I saw the doctors at the hospital.

Carl looked through my computer to try and find my name. He found no files, not even a journal, although he did get excited when he saw the hard-drive icon had the name Lily White underneath it. But I knew that was not my name. It is the computer's name. Seemed obvious to me. He looked under the internet preferences, where my name and e-mail address should have been, but they were blank.

"I don't know much about Apples," Carl told me, "so something could be hidden someplace, but it seems as though everything was purposefully wiped out. The police could probably find out something, I guess, though I know Ronny is their computer expert, and he don't know jack."

"No," I said. I did not want the police to have Lily White. So somehow we all forgot to tell the police about the computer when they came to the hospital to see me.

The doctor and nurse fixed up my battered feet, said I had not been sexually assaulted but I was a bit malnourished; otherwise I was healthy—couldn't explain the memory loss.

"What do you remember?" they asked.

"I don't know. I remember hearing the mountain whisper to me and waking up. Then Carl and Mary came through the mist."

Police said they had no bulletins or alerts regarding someone like me, although they had been having trouble with their computers and phone lines. A freak snowstorm had shut down everything south of Taos.

"Kind of convenient, this storm," Carl said, sitting in the chair next to me.

"What do you mean?"

"If there's gonna be a freak storm," Carl said, "or any snowstorm at all, it'll be here. We're at a higher elevation. But everything is closed down south of here. I bet what's chasin' you is south of here."

"Someone's chasing me?" I didn't like that.

"Metaphorically speaking," he said.

"You're saying I caused the storm?"

"I saw your wings, Angel," he said. "I know what you are aspiring to be. And I admire it. I wish I myself could be angelic, but it's not in my nature."

I couldn't help but giggle.

"What?" Carl asked.

"I was trying to picture you with wings," I said. "What do you mean you saw my wings?" I looked over my shoulder. "I don't see anything."

"I know," he said. "And that should be troublin'. But it's not. Angel wings are not the strangest thing we've ever seen here."

"Really?"

He nodded, then lowered his voice. "Some people think UFOs land here. Not me, of course, but I keep an open mind. The odds we humans are here on this planet at all are astronomical. Literally. So who knows what other long shots have turned out? Maybe you're an alien. Maybe I am. Can you keep a secret?"

"I don't know."

"Good point." He got up, went into the office, returned with a book. "Outside—I'll show you later— there's this petroglyph rock. It was put there by the Tiwa Indians." He opened the book and read, "'To help anchor the energy of Pueblo Mountain, from whose Blue Lake they trace their origin as a tribe.'" He looked at me. "But here's the secret part." He read again, "'It has been used as a navigational guide for extraterrestrial visitors because the site also marks the entranceway to other dimensions.'" He tapped the book, then handed it to me. "See, it's right there."

I looked at the gray photograph of the rock. "Carl."

"Yep?"

"It can't be much of a secret if it's here in this book."

"Well, you've got a point there, little alien-slash-angel-child."

I laughed.

"You can read that if you want. Tell you all about this house. Mabel Dodge Luhan and Tony Luhan made this place. Mabel wanted to find a spot she could call home where beauty, art, and nature intersected."

I looked at the cover. *Utopian Vistas: The Mabel Dodge Luhan House and the American Counterculture,* by Lois Palken Rudnick.

"Did she find it here? A home?"

"I think so."

"Is this your home?"

"The Big House?" He shook his head. "No, I just work here. I live right over there in the Gate House. You see, Mabel had money. She could afford angst. Could afford to look around. This is where I was born. I did some wandering when I was young, even though I couldn't afford it, and ended up back here. So yeah, I guess it is home. Dennis Hopper used to own this place."

"Who?" I asked.

"I hope that's your amnesia talking and not the ignorance of youth."

I flipped through the book and stopped at a quote from Susan Sontag. "'The felt unreliability of human experience brought about by the inhuman acceleration of historical change has led every sensitive modern mind to the recording of some kind of nausea, of intellectual vertigo. And the only way to cure this spiritual nausea seems to be, at least initially, to exacerbate it.'"

"Or amnesia," Carl said. "Maybe you've got amnesia instead of vertigo—you know, because of modern life—so you need to exacerbate it. Be even more forgetful. Don't try to remember."

"You know, Carl, that actually makes sense to me. But I'm already forgetting what you said."

They put me in the Austin Room. I can see the Sacred Mountains from a tiny window in the bedroom. There's also a big bathroom with a claw-foot tub.

I didn't know who Mary Austin was. When I asked Mary, she said, "A white woman who lived in Santa Fe. She was a writer, a friend to Mabel Dodge." She answered as she made the bed. "Is it warm enough in here for you? If you get too cold, you can adjust the heat from the office." When Mary finished, she stood, her hands folded over her belly, and looked around the room.

"I'll be all right," I told her.

Mary did not look at me.

"I'm not afraid," I said.

"Your mother will come for you soon," Mary said.

"Do you think I have a mother? Carl thinks I'm an angel or an alien."

"Carl talks too much."

"But he's funny."

Mary smiled slightly. "I could stay."

I shook my head.

"Remember," Mary said, "you are supposed to stay off your feet as much as possible."

"OK."

I like Mary. She made me dinner when we came back from the hospital. Refried beans. Steamed vegetables. A little bit of chicken. Guacamole. At first I could only stare at it. Something about it made me nervous. So she handed me an apple.

"This will prepare your belly," she said.

"This apple is so red," I said. "I don't remember seeing anything quite this red. Is it really all right if I eat it? If I do, won't I then be part apple and part me? Whoever that is."

"It is good to eat the apple," Mary said.

"This apple tastes like water and . . . sweetness," I said.

Then I ate the rest of the food, slowly, chewing every bite many times. Mary cleaned around me as I sat at the table in the middle of the kitchen.

Now I am alone. I want to sleep, but my back itches. I am still not afraid. Or worried. "Ignorance is bliss" is what Carl says. I guess he's right.

. . . .

Carl knocked on my door, then came in with a breakfast tray. "The guests are eating," he said, "but we thought you should stay off your feet." I sat in the rocking chair next to the bed.

"Look," I said. I held up my bare feet. The bandages were gone, my skin pink.

Carl looked like he was going to drop the tray. He set it on the bed, then squatted near my feet.

"I can only say wow," he said.

He had seen my feet when they were swollen, scratched, bruised, and bleeding.

"What happened?"

"I don't know," I said. "As I was falling to sleep, I wished my feet were better so that I could walk around the place."

"You got the power, girl. The roads are all closed between here and Santa Fe," he said. "Ice and snow." He opened my curtains. I went over to the window and looked out at the courtyard. The huge, old cottonwoods, their branches still dressed beautifully in nearly heart-shaped golden leaves, moved like dancers in the wind. The sunlight streaming through them made the entire courtyard golden and the adobe rose colored.

"This is beautiful," I said. "Can I stay here?"

"Ain't up to me, girl," Carl said. "We need to find your parents. I bet they're worried shitless."

"But it's so peaceful here," I said.

"Eat your breakfast," he said.

I turned around, sat cross-legged on the bed, and began to eat. Carl sat in the rocking chair.

"White people come to New Mexico and always romanticize everything," he said. "The colors, the light, the Pueblo. That's what Mabel did, in a way. She wanted to bring together artists and thinkers of her day and meld what they had to offer with the culture of the Taos Pueblo."

"And that didn't work?" I asked. The eggs were creamy. Some kind of spice or something I could not identify.

"No," he said. "New Mexico is like a third-world country in many ways. The poverty rate is incredible. Yet all these rich people run around paying outrageous prices for artwork—artwork that sits in warehouses and no one ever gets to see. No one is ever moved by it. It's just a commodity. A business."

My stomach started to hurt. I put my fork down.

"Oh, sorry. Shouldn't be talking about this shit while you're eating. Go ahead." He nodded toward my plate. "No place is perfect. I'm just jawing. Mary says I talk way too much. She told me just to bring you your food and shut up. So go ahead and eat. Then I'll show you the petroglyph rock."

Someone knocked at the front door. Carl got up and opened it. Mary came in.

part four

"I better get to work," Carl said. "I'll catch you later."

"The police just called," Mary said. "They think they have found your parents. They gave me a number you can call to talk to them."

"The police or the parents?" I asked.

"The parents," Mary said.

I'm sitting outside underneath the portico in front of my room. The wind through the dry leaves is kind of spooky and beautiful at the same time. The light is still golden. I feel cocooned.

The phone number is in my pants pocket. Natasha's pants pocket. She brought me a few changes of clothes. I look down at the huge stones that make up the floor of the courtyard. Some of them have been cemented in place, probably to keep people from tripping and falling on them. Two handprints have been pressed into the wet cement and are now solid, with names scribbled in the cement below them. One hand is small, the other bigger. I get up, move closer to the hands, then squat by them.

Underneath the little hand—the left hand—the name Mercy is scratched. The adult hand—the right hand—has the name Nancy beneath it. I stretch my left hand out and press it into the child's hand. My hand is too big. I place my right hand into Nancy's hand.

Perfect fit.

I sigh. I should call those people, whoever they are.

"Hey, Angel, come on over."

I look up. Carl is a few yards away, nearer to the cottonwoods, motioning to me. I get up and walk to him. He points to a gray stone that's about three feet by two feet by one. It looks like an ordinary stone.

"This is it," Carl says, sitting on the rock. "Some believe this is the doorway to another dimension."

I sit next to him.

"Do you feel any different?" *he asks.*

"I feel comfortable," *I say.* "Yes, it feels really nice sitting here."

"But you don't see lights or hear anything unusual?" *he asks.*

"No," *I say.* "Do you?"

He shakes his head. "I never have. At least as far as I can remember. Sometimes I think I have what they call lost time, but then, that could just be a hangover. Let me show you something else."

We get up and he takes me to a kind of porch over a tiny stream. We sit in chairs on the porch.

"This is the Acequia Madre, the Mother Ditch. Everyone shares responsibility for this water. We clean it up in the spring, and we let the majordomo know how much water we need and when to irrigate crops."

We sit in silence, me listening to the water flow beneath us.

I know the answer before I ask the question, but I ask it anyway. "Is this the way of the world? Everyone working together?"

Carl shrugs. "Some places. Mary Austin said that 'rain falls on radical and conservative alike, but the mother ditch makes communists of them all.' She thought this kind of cooperation would bring about peace and stability. Mother-rule, she called it. Lots of* *people have called this land—New Mexico—women's land. Mary Austin and Mabel Dodge were 'daughters of the desert.' Maybe you are too. That's where we found you."*

"What would it mean to be a daughter of the desert?" I ask.

"What do you think?"

"Well, if I was like Mabel and Mary, I suppose it would mean that this place felt like home. And I'd be an idealist. I'd still believe people could get it right."

"Does that describe you?"

"I don't know. You'll have to ask my parents when they come."

"Mercy? We've been terrified!" the woman on the other end of the line was crying.

"Mercy." A man's voice. "The roads are closed. We can't get up there. And no one will fly us in either. Not from here."

"I don't know you," I said.

The man cleared his throat. "We understand that. We've talked to the doctor. He doesn't think you've had any physical trauma, so that's good. You'll get your memory back. We'll come as soon as we can. We checked your e-mail, and you had e-mailed your journal to yourself, from some Wi-Fi site. Do you remember doing that?"

"No," I said. "In fact, I don't know what you're talking about. What makes you think I'm your daughter?"

"I recognize your voice," the man said. "And the police faxed us your photograph. You've got photographs on your computer of us—of all of us together."

"We couldn't find anything like that."

I didn't know what else to say.

"I like it here," I finally said.

"We'll come up there as soon as we can. If you don't want to call us Mom and Dad, my name is George and your mother is Nancy."

"I don't think I want to leave here."

George hesitated. "You've only been there a few hours, haven't you?"

"A day," I said. "You can just sit and listen to the trees. Artists and writers have been coming here forever. Well, for the last eighty years or so. And it's right next to Pueblo land. The Pueblo has been here for over four hundred years. Without any electricity or plumbing. They don't even have to filter the water from the stream to use it. It's very peaceful."

"Can we come up and join you, then?"

I hesitated.

"No more doctors," I said.

"Okay," George said. "We'll be there as soon as they open the roads."

Mary had to run some errands at the Pueblo, so I went with her. First she bought me a pair of tennis shoes. At the Pueblo she told me she would return soon, and then she walked away, leaving me by the entrance. The woman in the little house at the gate nodded to me, then turned her attention to a group needing to pay to get in. The sun was out. No wind. The Pueblo "apartment house" looked so familiar, the clustered adobe buildings with ladders sticking out here and there. I had probably seen them in books and on postcards. Dogs ran around everywhere, but none barked. Dried poop lay on the bare blond dirt. I walked over to the river that ran through the village. I sat at the edge of it, on a patch of grass.

I closed my eyes. It was so quiet. I heard no traffic. Felt no pulse of electricity.

Bliss.

I heard the flutter of wings and looked up.

A crow flew overhead.

I smiled.

Later I watch Mary cook. She does not let me watch for long. It is some kind of soup, and she has Carl and I chopping vegetables. She doesn't say much, but Carl talks a lot. He's funny. Neither of them seems to worry about anything.

After they leave, I can't sleep. I stare out into the darkness, then walk across the courtyard to the petroglyph rock. Carl says sometimes he comes out here and sits on it to see if he can go to another dimension. So far he hasn't gone anywhere else—at least not anywhere he can consciously remember, he adds. I sit on the stone and look up at the stars. I don't feel anything different or otherdimensional. Except my butt gets cold. It is beautiful and serene, sitting here looking up at the sky. Eventually I go back inside.

I dream of wings. Discarded wings, spread out all over the desert. When I awaken, I am crying.

"Mercy!" The woman who said she was my mother embraced me so tightly I could hardly breathe.

Carl and Mary left us alone in the Big Room. I wanted to run after them.

The man gave me a quick hug. Then we all sat on the sofa.

"You look good," Nancy said.

"You look tired," I said.

"We've been very worried," Nancy said. "Do you remember anything yet?"

I shook my head.

"I really think it would be best if we took you to a hospital," Nancy said. "And got you a full workup."

"They said here there's nothing wrong with me."

"Obviously there is something wrong with you if you can't remember who you are," Nancy said gently.

"They call me Angel here."

"I don't think that's a good idea," George said. "You're not an angel."

"No one said I was," I said. "Did they?"

Nancy bit her lip.

"Do I have brothers and sisters?" I asked.

"No," George said.

"But you have a grandmother who is very worried

about you," Nancy said. "Aunt Lenny is too. Grandma Dottie is flying up here tomorrow, if the weather is better."

"When did you last see me?" I asked.

George cleared his throat again. "Just the day before you went missing. You were at a treatment center."

"What kind of treatment center? Drugs? I do drugs?"

George shook his head. "For eating disorders."

"Are you eating here?" Nancy asked.

"Yes," I answered.

"Good," she said.

I frowned.

"Do you need to check into your hotel?" I asked. Anything to get them to go away.

"No," Nancy said. "We've got rooms here. We'll stay here until you're ready to go home."

"This is home," I said.

"No, it's not," Nancy said. "You've only been here two days. How can you think this is home?"

George stood. "Maybe we should go check in, unpack. We can meet with Mercy again in a little bit."

Nancy looked like she wanted to say something, but she didn't. She nodded and got up. "We'll see you in a little while?" she asked.

"I'll be here."

"Oh." Nancy stopped and dug something out of her pocket and handed it to me. It was a *mala.* I remembered what a *mala* was. I took it from her. The beads felt cool to my touch. "You left this at the treatment center. Aunt Lenny, my sister, gave it to you before you went away."

"*Om Tara tu tare ture soha,*" I whispered.

"You remember?" Nancy asked.

"I guess so."

I went over to the Guest House, a hop, a skip, and a walk on the path away from the Big House, where Carl was working on some electrical problem. The radio was up so loud he didn't hear me come in. Then he jumped when he saw me.

"Little cat's feet, eh?" he said, turning down the radio. "Led Zeppelin. You remember them?"

"Some ancient rock group, right?" I asked, smiling.

"You're a sly one, you." He crouched down to the electrical outlet again. "I'm working on this project about Led Zeppelin. I believe we can find answers to all of life's questions in Led Zeppelin's songs. You know, the way people say Shakespeare or the Bible has all the answers. Led Zeppelin is our modern answer to Shakespeare. I'm trying to arrange the thing by the question. Like, say you had a love problem. Then, I would glean quotes from their songs to address that problem."

I sat on the floor near him. "So how's the project going?"

He shrugged. "They sing a lot about sex."

I laughed.

"But then, I've always believed—before starting on this project—that rock 'n' roll was about one thing: sex. Course, in our day sex was a lot simpler."

"What do you mean?"

"It was before AIDS," he said, pulling on something inside the outlet. I hoped he knew what he was doing. "You kids have a whole lot more things to think about than just about whether someone's going to get knocked up or something."

"What's AIDS?" I asked.

He looked over at me. "You have a very selective amnesia, don't you?"

"How would I know!"

"How'd you like your parents?"

I shrugged. "He seemed lost, and she seemed pissed off."

"You don't really look like either of them," he said. "But then, I don't look like my parents either. We're just conglomerations of all our ancestors, aren't we?"

I heard Nancy and Mary talking in the kitchen. I didn't mean to eavesdrop. Well, actually, I did. I had seen my mother earlier, sitting out back near the outside oven. She had her elbows on the table, her head in her hands, and she was crying. I felt so bad for her. Soon after she came into the house. I waited, then followed her. I didn't want to talk to her, but I wanted to know what she was saying. I sat at the dining-room table. They couldn't see me, but I could hear them.

"She's always been a very responsible child," Nancy said. "I'm a lawyer, and I'd come home telling all these awful stories. I should have been more circumspect, but I figured it was good for her to know what was going on in the world. We were here once before."

"Here at this house?" Mary asked. I could hear her moving something around, back and forth. Was it bread dough?

"Yes," Nancy said. "Right after Mercy's brother was stillborn and my father died. She doesn't remember coming here, for some reason. Never has. I just thought it was because she was so young when we visited. I loved it here. I started crying almost the moment we got here. It was so nice to be someplace where beauty mattered, after all these court battles over the environment. Trying to explain to these judges and lawyers and businesspeople that the land is sacred—nature is sacred—is almost impossible. Maybe Mercy doesn't remember because I cried so much. But I wasn't unhappy, I was just feeling it all."

I couldn't quite grasp the idea that I had been here before and didn't remember it. And a brother and grandpa, both dead?

"She was with her grandpa when he died," Nancy said. "We all were. But he looked her in the eyes just before he died and said, 'You look after your mother and grandmother *for me.' And then he died. You can't do that to a six-year-old. But he said it before I could stop him, and he was dying. What could I say? I explained to her later that she was not responsible for us, and she seemed all right. But who knows? And now all this stuff about her having wings."*

"Wings?" Mary asked.

"Before she ran away from the treatment center," Nancy said, "she told us she was an angel and she didn't need to eat. She said she could feel the wings growing on her back. We took her to a doctor, but they didn't find anything either. We wanted to make sure, you know, that there wasn't really something going on."

I got up and went back outside quietly. On little cat's feet. Then I reached my hands behind me and tried to feel my back. No wings. Just bone, skin, some muscle.

I went around to the front of the house, to the spot where I had seen little Mercy's handprint. I crouched down near the hands again. I put mine in Nancy's.

"Do you remember when we did these?"

I looked up. My mother sat on the ground next to me.

"No," I said.

"You were so excited," she said. "It was in the fall too, I think. The cottonwood leaves floated down from the trees, like pieces of gold being slowly released from a sky-held treasure chest. You stood in the middle of the courtyard, spinning around, laughing, your hands stretched out. It was such a beautiful sight. Ecstasy personified. Later they were doing this, and you and I sneaked over and put our handprints in the cement."

"Did you dance with me?" I asked.

"I don't remember," she said. "Probably. Most certainly. Wouldn't I?" She shrugged.

"I had a brother?"

"Not really," she said. "He died before he was born. Peter."

"He was still my brother," I said. "Just like he was your son."

She flinched slightly, then said, "Yes, of course he was your brother." She looked away from me. "I was arguing a case when I was pregnant with him. It was a pretty horrendous case of poisoning by a multinational corporation. They had allowed mercury tracings to seep into this town's water supply. Every day we heard testimony of one horror story after another of the damage done to those poor little bodies because they drank the water. Sometimes I thought Peter just couldn't stand this litany of horrors and decided to call it quits before he started."

"That must have felt really bad," I said.

Nancy looked over at me. "There I go again. Telling you all these horrible stories."

"But how can the truth be harmful?" I asked.

"That's what I always believed," Nancy said. "How could the truth be harmful? Perhaps there are many truths."

"I don't see how that's possible," I said. "The truth is the truth."

She smiled and smoothed my hair gently off my forehead.
"You'd think, wouldn't you?"

"Now, how do you play this again?" I asked. "When you put down an eight, you can change it to any suit?"

"That's why they call it crazy eights, sister," Carl said, slapping a six of spades on my mother's six of hearts.

"Don't let her fool you, Carl," George said as he played a card. "She always feigns memory loss when it comes to cards, and then she beats us all."

"A sly one," Carl said. "I knew it."

We sat at the dining-room table, the lights down low. Mary and Natasha had gone home. The few other guests were out or asleep.

I put down a two of spades. "Pick up two."

My mother made a face, then picked up two from the pile.

"So Dennis Hopper owned this place?" George said, glancing around.

"Yep. I suspect quite a bit of partying went on here," Carl said.

"Were you here then?" I asked.

"No, them was my wandering days," he said. "Which I don't remember a lot about, since I was doing my fair share of drugs myself."

"So you have amnesia too?" I said, grinning at him.

"Yeah, that's it."

"I never did drugs," Nancy said. "Didn't like the idea of being out of control. I drank too much, though. Until I met George. Then I straightened up."

"I took LSD once," George said, "just to see. The hallucinations were interesting, but I knew none of it was real. I never needed to do it again. I never liked drinking, and I still can't imagine smoking anything."

"Good for you, Dad," I said.

He made a noise. "Maybe not. Maybe I was too cautious."

"It wasn't caution," Nancy said. "It was disinterest. I hope you are equally disinterested, Mercy."

I shrugged. "How would I know?"

The adults looked at one another, then burst out laughing.

"Carl Jung visited here," my dad told me as we sat in the dark Rainbow Room. "Georgia O'Keeffe. Willa Cather. Ansel Adams. Mary Austin. Do you recognize any of those names?"

"Yep," I said. "All of them. Do you think our Carl is a descendant of Carl Jung?"

"That would be very synchronicitious, wouldn't it?" he said.

I laughed. "Dad, I don't think that's a word."

Carl took us to the upstairs bathroom.

"What?" I asked, looking around. The room was

dominated by colorful paintings on the glass windows. A star. Sun. Other things I did not recognize. Was that because I had forgotten what they were?

"These windows," Carl said, "were painted by D. H. Lawrence."

"Very cool," I said.

George reached out and touched one of the panes. "I had forgotten about these. I don't think we got to see them last time we were here."

"Lawrence said he liked America because we had no past," Carl said. "He was speaking of white America, of course. He thought we should align ourselves with aboriginal ways. 'They must catch the pulse of life which Cortés and Columbus murdered.' That was what Mabel was trying to do, I think. But Lawrence didn't particularly like her, from what I can understand, and thought New Mexico was too dominated by women. Least, that's my interpretation, gleaned through my reading of everyone else's interpretations." He grinned.

Dad and Mom laughed.

"Did Franz Kafka ever come here?" I asked.

"Kafka? What made you think of him?" Dad asked.

"I don't know."

"Naw. I think he was dead by the time Mabel got here. Would have been cool, though, eh? If he had written about waking up as a bug here, what kind of bug do you think it would have been? A scorpion?

Wasp? Or would it have been an animal? Like the coyote."

"I'm going to bed," Mom said.

"Wait," I said. "Carl. Let's show them the rock."

"I don't know, sister," he said, shaking his head as we walked down the steep, narrow staircase. "What if *they* decide to come just then and take them away?"

"Well, then I wouldn't have to leave here," I said.

"Hey," Mom said.

I laughed and ran outside. It had gotten cold, and I needed my jacket. But I didn't care. I ran to the rock and impatiently motioned the three adults over to me. "Sit, sit. The aliens use this as an anchor or beacon or something. It's a threshold into other dimensions."

We each took a place on the stone. Dad rubbed my shoulders to keep me warm. We squirmed and giggled and gazed at the sky.

We saw a falling star.

"Quick," I said, "breathe in the stardust so we can live forever."

I dreamed I put one hand in little Mercy's cement imprint and the other in my mother's. Both fit. The red earth suddenly poured up through my fingers, like red Earth hands, and grasped my hands. "This is home," I heard someone whisper. In a voice that sounded just like mine. "Home."

. . . .

My mom and I sit on the Adirondack chairs underneath the portico. Dad left to pick up Grandma early this morning. I still don't remember them being my parents or my life before here, but it seems OK to spend time with them. I read Utopian Vistas, *and Mom closes her eyes and stretches her legs out in front of her. She looks better this morning.*

"I could stay here forever," she says.

"See?"

She chuckles. "You always think you're right," she says.

"So do you."

She laughs out loud. "Did you just figure that out, or are you remembering?"

"I figured it out."

"My granddaughter," Grandma Dottie said as Dad helped her walk across the courtyard. She held out her arms for me. I ran into them.

She stroked my hair as she held me. "Ah, you are getting some meat on your bones. Good, good." She let me go. "My daughter," she said to Mom, and mother and daughter embraced.

"Thanks for coming, Ma," Mom said. "We'll take you to your room."

Her room was next to mine, the Cather Room.

My father put his arm across my shoulders and squeezed me.

"Do you remember her?" he asked quietly.

I shook my head. "Not even a little."

While Grandma slept, Mary, Mom, and I made dinner. Carl brought over his Led Zeppelin bible notes to show my father. I wasn't sure he was actually interested, but he listened.

"Has to be mild for Mom," Nancy said.

So we made mild refried beans, tamales, potatoes, salad, and wild salmon. Standing in the kitchen did not feel familiar at all, but it was strangely comforting. After a while my mother seemed to stop noticing when I popped something into my mouth and ate it. The first time I did it, she got tears in her eyes. I thought, geez, I must have made these people miserable.

Mary stayed to supper, and the six of us sat at the main dining-room table, eating and talking. Dad was fascinated with life at the Pueblo, and I could see it was somewhat of a strain on Mary to keep answering his questions. A bit of a culture clash. To him it was polite to keep asking. I suspected for her it wasn't. Carl showed Mom and Grandma card tricks. He wasn't very good at them, and he kept having to show them over and over until he got it right.

After we finished eating and promised to clean up, Mary left to meet her husband, who had worked late that night. No other guests were staying in the inn, so Carl brought the radio out from the kitchen and switched it on. He found a rock 'n' roll station and turned it up—not too loud. He and Grandma got

148

up to dance to a slow song. She told him to make his spine straight and to hold her more firmly. I laughed. I came from a long line of bossy women.

I liked that.

My father took my mother in his arms, and they swept around the room, looking each other in the eyes.

They loved each other.

Tears started streaming down my cheeks. I let them fall. It was just so . . . joyful to watch such joy.

Love.

Living.

When the music got fast again, I got up and danced with them, while my grandmother sat down. After a while I went and sat with her. She let me help her up to the Big Room. We sat on one of the sofas together. We could still hear the music and the three dancers laughing.

"Now, tell me what's been happening," Grandma Dottie said, her accent still strong after all these years. She took my hand in hers.

"I don't remember much, Grandma."

"Your mother told me about your eating difficulty," she said. "And that you thought you were growing wings, becoming an angel, and you didn't think angels had to eat."

"That's what she told me, too," I said.

"What do you remember?"

"I remember being on the Hopi land, stretching my arms out to the Sacred Mountains, even though I didn't know what they

149

were or where I was. I heard this fluttering sound, like wings, then I saw Carl and Mary coming through a kind of mist—probably the mist of my mind."

She nodded. "Do you remember I was in a concentration camp when I was a girl just about your age?"

I shook my head. "What's a concentration camp?"

She looked into my eyes. "It is where the German Nazis sent Jews, dissidents, Gypsies, homosexuals, and others—mostly so we would die."

"That's horrible," I said. My stomach was beginning to hurt.

"I want to tell you something," she said. "I think I told you this when you were a girl, but I can't be so sure. I was in the camp for two years. I was one of the lucky ones. Our family, at least most of it, had been able to hide for a long time. We went to France finally, thinking we would be safe there, but we were not. We got shipped back to Germany and ended up in Ravensbrück. It was a camp in the German countryside, beautiful area. Horrible place. My sister and mother began starving almost immediately. I didn't. I don't know why I did all right and they did not. I gave them any extra food I could find or steal. A strange thing happened. All of us would look for any sign of life on the other side, you know. We hardly ever saw birds. Or heard anything except our own suffering. But soon after I got there, I would sometimes see what I thought was a hawk flying overhead. It was beautiful. Kind of golden brown, tip of red on its tail, I think. I was a city girl, so I didn't really know what it was. But I thought it was a hawk and that it was a miracle that *it was alive. I saw it every once in a while. Every time I did, I would hear a voice in my head say, 'Don't be afraid.' As you can imagine, this seemed a ridiculous thing to hear! There were many reasons to be afraid. But there was more to it. 'Don't be afraid, but pay attention.' And so I would, and something always came to pass. Sometimes the something was bad, sometimes helpful. I got used to hearing a kind of rustling or fluttering, like a bird taking off, and I would know I needed to pay attention. I might hear it and suddenly know where to get some extra food. Or it might be the night they were taking people to the gas chamber, and I'd find a place to hide and get to live another night. I felt like that hawk—or whatever it was—that bird saved my life many times. Sometimes I would close my eyes and imagine hundreds of birds, all different kinds, descending into the camp or springing from the muddy earth, the rocks, any place, and transforming us and the world."*

The house was suddenly quiet.

"So you don't think I am becoming an angel," I said.

"Maybe the angel was becoming you," she said. "I don't know. I know that sometimes the world seems so horrible that we cannot bear to be human beings any longer. We look at what is happening and can't figure out anything to do except to sacrifice our bodies—we don't eat enough, work too hard, push ourselves. But sweetheart, your body is the sweetest and best place to be in the world. You know, I kept going even in that horrible place, I stayed alive, for myself. I didn't do it for your mother or for you." She shrugged. "I may have thought of you from time to time. But I *wanted to be alive. I wanted to live every moment I could."*

"Because in spite of everything, you still believe that people are really good at heart?"

"You can quote Anne Frank, but you don't recognize your own grandmother? Tsk, tsk." She squeezed my hand. "I don't think goodness had anything to do with it. I just wanted to live, whatever that meant."

"You are braver than I am," I said. "I think I would want to die if I saw the world you saw."

She shook her head. "No, you wouldn't!"

"I don't feel so afraid when I'm here," I said. "Last night I dreamed I pressed my hand into the ground, and the Earth came up and held my hand just like you are and said, 'This is home.' I think it means I should stay here, don't you?"

Grandma held up my hand. "It means home is right here," she said, tapping my hand with her other hand. "In your body. Home is where you are. Everywhere is sacred, and everywhere is home—as long as you are there. Alive and present."

I rested my head against her shoulder. "Do you ever get angry, Grandma?"

She laughed, "Of course I do. If you aren't at least sometimes angry, you aren't really paying attention."

"Do you believe in God?" I asked.

"That is a good question," she said. "That hawk was like God to me for a time. It seemed to know things about my life. I suppose there could be a God. If there is, he's not doing a very good job. Too many terrible things have happened."

I closed my eyes. "I wish I could take away all your pain, Grandma."

"Who gave you permission to do that, my granddaughter? It's my pain."

We drove the Enchanted Circle, my parents and I, while Grandma stayed behind to nap. At some point we parked, got out of the car, and walked around. As I ducked under a juniper tree, I heard the fluttering of wings and looked up to see a crow flying overhead. "Ack, ack, ack," it said. Maybe it was a raven. Whichever, I waved.

I felt anxious. Irritated. My back itched.

At the house again, I went to take a nap. When I awakened, a small boy sat at the end of my bed.

"Who are you?"

"Peter!" he said sharply. "Your brother."

"I'm sorry," I said. "I've lost my memory. Did something bad happen to me that I can't remember?"

"Something bad happens to all of us," he said.

I gasped and opened my eyes. The little boy was gone.

I heard the fluttering of wings and knew something was happening.

"Bluebird is driving the girls up from Mercywood," Mom said at breakfast.

Bluebird. She was from the treatment center. Had

graduated. Did I remember that or had my mother told me?

My stomach lurched.

"How long was I missing?" I asked.

"Four days," my father said.

"What do you think I was doing for four days?" I asked.

"We hope you'll be able to tell us," Nancy said.

"Do you think it was something bad?" I asked.

Grandma looked up from her food.

"Of course it was not bad! You were being taken care of," she said. "You know, we forget many things in our lives. I don't remember most of what happened to me in the camp. That is a blessing!"

"But if we forget, aren't we doomed to repeat the past?" I asked. "Isn't that what they always say?"

"I remember enough," Grandma said. "And you remember enough."

"I don't remember anything!" I said.

"That is enough for now!"

"Ma, you are speaking in riddles," my mother said.

"She's the Delphic oracle," Dad said. "High on bay leaf fumes. She makes perfect sense to me. Mercy will remember when she needs to remember."

Carl hopped down the steps to us.

"Your friends just drove up," he said. "Would you like to come out and see them?"

I did not feel well. Wanted to throw up. What was happening?

"You were quite fond of them," my mother said.

I pushed away from the table, the chair scraping across the floor noisily. I ran up the steps and went outside.

I breathed deeply.

Everything is all right. Everything is all right.

I walked across the courtyard.

Bluebird bounced up the steps.

"Hello!" she cried, putting her arms around me.

I recognized her.

"How's the outside?" I asked.

"I don't know, girl, how's it with you? Good thing my folks were out of town, eh, so I could hide you for a few days."

"You?"

"Nice digs." Mia got out of the car next. "Heard you don't remember anything? Geez. How could you forget me?" She spun around.

"Where's Snapshot?"

Bluebird nodded toward the car.

I hurried down the steps.

That sound again.

My back hurt. Was I really growing wings?

Or letting them go?

"Hey there, Tam-may!" Snapshot said. "Look who I brought with!"

She opened a car door. One skinny leg came out. Then another.

The rest of the body.
She smiled.
I gasped.
"Hello, darlin'," Suzy-Q said. She grinned.
I could not breathe.
"I . . . I thought you were dead," I stammered.
"Exaggerated, totally," Suzy-Q said.
"You gave her mouth-to-mouth," Snapshot said.
Suddenly it all came back to me.
All at once.
Every motherfucking thing.
Imagine. Everything you know.
Suddenly knowing it.
I screamed.
And screamed.
Girls starving themselves.
AIDS.
The Holocaust.
The Inquisition.
The Irish potato famine.
I was on my knees in the gravel. Could barely see.
"What's wrong with her?" someone said.
The suffragists dying as the authorities force-fed them.
Peter dead.
Grandpa, "Take care of your mother and grandmother."
I pulled myself up. Ran.
My mother gasping for breath.

One war after another.

One illness after another.

One death after another.

The Earth gasping for breath.

And ran.

Cadavers walking around like girls. And women.

Suzy-Q dropping to the floor. Sickening sound. Breathing her last breath.

Only. Only. I breathed it back into her. We went back and forth.

I had a responsibility. The ability to respond. I could bring her back from the dead. From the almost dead.

It wasn't because she had died that my memory had shattered.

It was that I had breathed life into her.

What if I hadn't been there? What if I hadn't thought of it? What if? What if? What if?

Look what happened all those times I was not around.

"Take care of your mother and grandmother."

I tried, Grandpa, but I haven't been able to. Mom still has trouble breathing. She's still sad. Peter is still dead. You're still dead.

I'm shivering even though Carl has put me in front of the fire. I'm in the Gate House. He called the Big House and told them where I was.

"You remembered?" he says.

I nod.

"Man, that's heavy. All at once like that. Shit. Good thing you've had a good life."

"What are you talking about?" I say. "My brother's dead. My mother can't breathe because the environment is so fucked up. My grandmother survived a Nazi concentration camp."

"But you're all right," he says. "It didn't happen to you."

"I feel like it has all happened to me," I say.

My mother is pounding on the door. Carl opens it and she comes inside.

"You remembered?"

She sits next to me, and I move away from her slightly.

"Did you know fourteen million children are AIDS orphans?" I ask. "Did you know that we've got about ten years, if that, to turn around the environment before it goes to hell in a handbasket?"

"It's already gone there, sister," Carl says.

"And I can't do anything about it!" I say.

"We all do what we can," Mom says.

"But we don't! I felt like I had to save it all, fix it all, because no one else is doing anything! But I don't know how to help anything either."

"If you were an angel, you figured you'd have some kind of magical powers?" she asks. She is trying not to cry. Trying to keep her breath.

"Well, I would have a better chance of making a difference."

"I hear ya, sister," Carl says.

"But . . ."

"But?" Mom asks.

"I'm not an angel. I'm just a girl."

"Yes, darlin'," Mom says. "You are just a girl, and that's all you need to be." She opens her arms and I fall into them. She holds me tightly but not too.

I sigh. Tremble. Or is that Mom?

Is that fluttering I hear again?

I look around the room. Carl has several shelves of videos and DVDs.

"You wanna watch a movie?" he asks.

"While the world dissolves around me?"

"Why not?" Mom says.

"Here, I'll pick one for you," Carl says. "I'll close my eyes and just pick one. Jung's way. Synchronicity."

He pulls a video off the shelf and shows it to us. King of Hearts. *I laugh.*

"I just told the girls about that movie," I say.

"You and my dad watched that movie together," Mom says. "At least a couple of times."

"I remember the movie," I say. "But I didn't know I watched it with Grandpa. You, me, and Dad went to a campus theater and saw it when I was younger."

"I remember," Mom says. "You cried."

"So did you."

Carl puts the video in the machine, then he leaves.

"Grandpa used to call you his Little Princess of Hearts," Mom

says. "He said that when you grew up, you would be the Queen of Hearts!"

I shake. "He had a lot of faith in me."

"He loved you," Mom says. "You were princess of his heart. Whenever he started getting depressed about what he had seen when they liberated the camp or what was happening in the world, he looked at you."

I look down at my hands.

"That doesn't mean you have to fix everything for everyone," Mom says. "It just means he loved you. We all love you. That doesn't mean you have to save us."

Mom and I watch the video. Eventually I sink out of my mother's arms and fall to sleep with my head in her lap, her stroking my hair. I wake up, watch more movie, fall to sleep. I dream. I steal my grandmother away from the concentration camp. Peter and I run through the French town, the ballerina dancing before us. Birds flutter overhead. The Fab Five mingle with the lunatics, eating at banquet after banquet. Mom and Dad dance. All my grandparents, too.

We all end up at the lunatic asylum together with the naked Scottish soldier.

"So everything turned out," I say, sitting up at the end of the movie.

"Well, there was still a war, and they were still in a lunatic asylum," Mom says.

"But they decided how they would live," I say.

"Exactly."

I nod.

"Terrible things happen, sugar," Mom says. "And you can't fix most of them. Maybe not any of them. But this is what I believe: If you don't at least try to live in joy, to dance, to love ecstatically, then the bastards win."

"I don't have to save the world?" Just because I saved Suzy-Q doesn't mean I have to save everyone.

"Do you know how you would save the world?"

I shake my head. "When I was a girl, I believed I was put on this earth to love. That was it. Then I got older and realized that was kind of foolish."

"A fool is just a person at the beginning of a journey," Mom says. "Dad and Mary are making dinner. You ready to go back and eat?"

"Yeah, I'm ready to eat."

My mother and I walked back to the house, holding hands. The house was lit by sweet light. As I walked toward it, I was certain anything could happen. I stood in the doorway for a moment before I stepped into the dining room.

Everyone was crowded around one table. Steam rose from the dishes on the table, and Carl, Dad, and Mary were still bringing food out from the kitchen. It smelled of beauty, ecstasy, joy.

Snapshot looked over and saw Mom and me.

"What happened?" Snapshot asked.

Mom and I walked into the dining room.

"Isn't all this food disgusting?" Bluebird said.

"Yeah, and you better eat everything on your plate," I said. "And no one better fucking throw up afterward."

"Mercy!" Grandma Dottie said.

"Sorry, Grandma."

"I've never seen so much food in my life," Suzy-Q said.

Corn on the cob, potatoes, glazed carrots, enchiladas, tamales, chicken, pork chops, fish, apple pie, burritos, scrambled eggs.

"Wow," Carl said, rubbing his hands together.

"It's all organic," Dad said. "Even the dead animals, which were all treated humanely before they were brutally slaughtered."

"Dad, we're trying to get people to *eat* . . . these brutally slaughtered creatures."

I stood and looked around the table. "Well, I would like to thank the spirits and beings of this place and the human beans." I glanced at my mother, and she smiled. "I thank them for this wonderful feast. I'm glad I'm alive to enjoy it. Thanks for surviving, Grandma." My throat tightened. "You too, Mom. And Dad. Thanks for having sex."

Everyone laughed.

"Now, dig in," I said.

The Fab Four did a great job of pretending to eat— if they were pretending. Suzy-Q and Bluebird actually put food in their mouths. Not much, but some.

"Hey, I saw heaven," Suzy-Q said. "There wasn't any food there, so I thought, better live it up while I can. Mercy, your dad said he would fly us all out to Oregon for Thanksgiving. Wouldn't that be a blast?"

"We're going to the ocean?" I asked.

"If you want to," he said.

"That would be so much fun!"

"It might be cold," Dad said, "and rainy."

"That's all right," I said. "I just want to see it."

"Where have you and your mom been?" Grandma Dottie asked.

"We watched a movie," I said. "Guess which one, girls?"

"*No,*" Suzy-Q said.

I nodded. "*King of Hearts*! It was great."

"Your grandfather loved that movie," Grandma Dottie said. "A great antiwar movie."

Suddenly the near-night light changed. The clouds had moved away from the sun, and gold and rose light suffused the outdoors. We all stood and went through various doors to the outside. I went up to the Big Room and out the front door to the courtyard. A breeze blew through the tops of the cottonwoods, and the golden leaves floated to the ground. I stood in the center of the courtyard, my arms spread out, and began turning in circles.

My mother clapped.

I glanced over at her as I spun around, feeling slightly dizzy. Grandma was next to her.

"Mom, Grandma! Come out. Dance with me!"

The two women stepped away from the portico, spread their arms wide, and turned as the leaves floated down all around them. The light was golden red on their faces. My mother smiled widely and closed her eyes. She began dancing in circles. My grandmother winked at me and spun around. She closed her eyes too.

I had never seen anything as beautiful as my mother and grandmother dancing with me while the cottonwood leaves fell all around us. I heard the fluttering of wings. Then, just before the almost heart-shaped cottonwood leaves touched the ground, they burst into feathers—into golden birds that flew all around us, until the courtyard was filled with us and golden birds breaking free, flying this way and that. My grandmother clapped her hands. She was a young girl again, joyful. And there was my grandpa Max, watching her, seeing her before all the pain.

Ahhh, ecstasy!

I closed my eyes for an instant.

When I opened them again, Suzy-Q, Mia, Snapshot, Bluebird, Dad, Carl, and Mary had joined us. Peter and Sandy were there too, dancing, laughing. Grandpa Max danced with Grandma Dottie.

They were all golden, all beautiful.

"Hey, Queen of Hearts," Suzy-Q said. "Your food is getting cold."

"Just another minute," I said. "Then we can go inside."